LOVE TRADE

LOVE TRADE

THE RISKY LOVERS SERIES, BOOK 1

MALLORY RUSH

ePublishingWorks!
love what you read.

Book and cover design by eBook Prep
www.ebookprep.com

March, 2020
ISBN: 978-1-64457-079-1

ePublishing Works!
644 Shrewsbury Commons Ave
Ste 249
Shrewsbury PA 17361
United States of America

www.epublishingworks.com
Phone: 866-846-5123

For Khosi Shongee
Now. And then.

DEAR READER...

Many years ago I wrote a book titled *Love Slave* that my Loveswept editors deemed too shocking to publish. That book found a home at Harlequin Temptation, was an *Editor's Choice* selection, became my first Mallory Rush novel in 1993, and was globally published, enjoying many foreign translations.

When I recently reread *Love Slave*, I decided 25 years may have made a big difference in what constitutes "shocking" but time had not encroached on the story's relevance—even if there were areas that could use some (okay, a LOT of) improvement. While the time frame was best left alone, and the heart of the story remains unchanged, the extent of edits and additions to the original material called for a new title.

I hope you enjoy *Love Trade*, now part of my Lovers & Lullabies series.

As always I love hearing from my readers and invite you to visit me at www.malloryrush.com. Wishing you a timeless supply of the kind of love you read about—

Mallory

PROLOGUE

"Time to say goodbye to your sister, Joshua." Mr. Johns patted the twelve-year-old boy's dark head.

Joshua stared hard at the social worker until the man glanced away uneasily, his Adam's apple bobbing up and down just like a turkey when he gobbled. Josh shrugged the comforting hand away. Didn't want no pity. Didn't want nobody but Sarah to even touch him.

"I gotta do this right," Joshua said quietly, so his little sister wouldn't hear. The man looked sad, even guilty. Josh played it for all it was worth. He stuck his thumb in the opposite direction, just like his daddy used to do when he sent him to his room. "Mr. Johns…please?"

Mr. Johns headed the other way, taking the grown-ups who'd accepted Sarah into their home along with him.

"C'mon, Sarah." Josh led the silent five-year-old into her new bedroom. She clutched her baby doll as Josh sat on the canopy bed and pulled Sarah onto his lap. "Let's talk," he said, tugging on a long blonde braid.

She didn't respond to his hair pulling but stared out the lace curtained window while she stroked her little hand through the doll's ratty curls.

"Remember the Christmas Santa brought you that?"

"There's no such thing as Santa Clause." She blinked her eyes and out rolled two big tears. "He's dead too."

"Now don't you start crying. If you do, you'll make me start and big boys don't cry. That's what Daddy always said. And we don't want to let him down. You and me, Sarah, we're gonna get through this and make him proud."

A huge sob shuddered through her small chest. Josh rocked her back and forth, the way he thought Daddy would do. And then he remembered his father telling him he was the man of the house and to watch after his sister while he went out for groceries that night he never came back.

"Oh, J-Josh," she stuttered out, "Josh, I'm sc-scared. I think I killed Daddy."

"That's crazy talk, Sarah."

"No it's not! 'Member when we got in trouble for laughing in church?"

"Yup. My butt's still stinging from the lick I got when we came home."

"'Cause you couldn't quit laughin' at the old lady singing in front. But I quit. Know how?"

"How?" Josh picked up a coverlet from the foot of the bed and wrapped it around them. He was going to miss tucking her in when he went to sleep in the strange bed at the orphanage he was getting dumped at. "How'd you quit laughing?"

"I pretended Daddy died. It was the horriblest, saddest thing I could think and it made me stop laughin'." She stared at him with big, frightened eyes while guilt and remorse contorted her impish face. "I did it other times too and now he's dead. I made him dead from thinkin' it. I'm a bad girl. A bad, bad girl. And preacher says the bad ones go down there. You know, that place where the devil's at with the brim and firestone? I don' wanna go there," she wailed. Sarah clutched the doll in her arms, twisting her fingers into the shaggy mop of hair.

"Shhh…shhh," he said, soothing her. "Now quit thinkin' like that, Sarah. You didn't make it happen and you're not gonna see any hellfire and brimstone. Don't go forgettin', you were always Daddy's angel, and you'll always be mine. Angels go to heaven, not hell."

"Josh, you know you're not 'sposed to say the H word. That'll earn you a lick for sure."

"And who's gonna give it to me? You?" He tweaked her nose and she giggled past her receding tears.

"You're sure I'm safe?" she asked hopefully.

"Absolutely, positively sure." Josh swallowed past a lump. They'd be coming for him soon, to take him away from Sarah. Then who would look at him as if he'd hung the moon? Mr. Johns? The warden at the orphanage in a neighboring county that had to be twenty miles away? Might as well be a hundred. A vision of iron bars and prison beds made him hug her tight.

"You're squishin' me, Josh!"

"Sorry." He forced himself to lessen his hold and fake an encouraging smile. "This is sure a pretty new room you've got, Sarah. Lots better than the one at home. They look real nice, your new folks do, and they were so excited when you got here, saying you were the little girl they'd always wanted."

"But they're not you. They're strangers and I want my daddy back."

"Me too. But that won't change nothin'. We've got to say good-bye for a little while but when I'm old enough I'm gonna take you away from here. That's a promise."

"When, Josh?"

He could visit on holidays. Big deal. He wanted his sister back and all he could think of now was years and years of more good-byes like this. It was tearing his guts out just thinking about it.

And so he didn't. He thought about how he was going to keep his promise to Sarah. He knew he'd need a place for them to live and enough money to take care of her.

How could he do it? Mowing lawns? But maybe the orphanage wouldn't even let him out to do that. Just like they'd lock him in tonight so he couldn't comfort Sarah while she cried herself to sleep.

Something hard knotted up inside him and settled protectively around his heart. His hands clenched the sheet and he held her as close as he could without making her yelp.

"I'll come back when I've got lots of money," he decided. "Then I'll buy you and me a brand-new house. Whenever you feel sad, just think about that."

"You promise?"

"Cross my heart, hope to—"

She threw her arms around his neck and nearly hugged the stuffings out of him. Josh stared at the window that was lifted a crack, the warm Mississippi breeze cutting through his emotions and clearing his head.

Suddenly, he had an answer, the beginnings of a plan.

"Can you keep a secret, Sarah? A real important secret? 'Cause if you tell, I can't come back to get you." She nodded her head, her braid bouncing up and down. "I'm running away."

"No, Josh! You could get in bad trouble."

"Only if they catch me." Realizing he didn't have any time to waste, he forced himself to put her down. His expression was stern. "This is what we've got to do. You lay down and pretend to be resting. If they ask you where I am, you say I went to get you a drink of water. That way they'll look around the house before they go after me."

"But that's lyin'!"

4

"It's a good lie, Sarah. If I don't get away I'll never be able to get you back and you want me to, don't you?"

"More'n anything." She looked real scared as Josh tucked her in and kissed her cheek. He was suddenly torn between crawling under the covers with her and making a run for it.

"I love you, Sarah. Be sure to say your prayers every night and remember you're my angel. And when you get homesick just think about me and that day I'll take you back home."

"I love you, big brother."

He extricated her arms from around his neck and gave her the baby doll to cling to instead. Josh turned before she saw the tears brimming in his eyes.

Big boys don't cry...big boys don't cry...

He crawled through the window then shut it back to a crack as soon as his feet touched grass. Blowing his sister a final kiss, he made sure the coast was clear then ran as fast as his feet could fly.

Sure wished he had some of those Keds so he could take off like Superman outrunning the train.

Train! He hadn't known where he was headed, but now he did. They'd passed some tracks a ways down the road. He'd hop the first train that whizzed by.

Josh was winded by the time he got there. He kept looking over his shoulder, expecting a pack of guard dogs to hunt him down once the alarm was sounded.

He'd followed the tracks a good mile when he heard a chug-a-lug that sounded like his own labored breathing. Then the train was passing, passing too fast and no way could he be Superman and outrun it. Just barely, he made out the oncoming blur of an open side-door.

Josh's legs pumped at top speed while he tried to remember how he'd seen this stowaway trick done in the movies. Only in the movies he'd be faster and taller, as tall as Sarah thought he was, tall enough to hang the moon and swing her on a star.

Do it! He sprang high at a dead run and caught the side edge of the partially opened railway car. The velocity of wind sucked at him, pulling him toward the slicing wheels and iron tracks. He screamed, his fingers sliding and clawing at the door's metal edge, desperately seeking enough hold to pull himself inside. As his body banged against the car Josh looked down, his eyes wild, terrified. He felt the mean steel all but eating up his feet and knew if he let go he'd be mangled like a mouse chewed up by a tomcat.

And then he felt something grab onto his locked arm. Raising his head, the wind whipped it so hard he thought his neck would snap. His eyes were glued to a grizzled face, a mouth gnashing out some urgent command.

He nearly pulled the man out with him before they were both safely inside. Josh fell into a trembling heap on the coarse floor. He heard the door being shoved nearly closed while the locomotive's deadly wheels sang a rusty lullaby against his raw cheek.

And then he was being gently nudged and a brown paper sack filled his stinging vision.

"Drink some, young'un. Not too much or you'll puke. Just a swig to make your innards quit shakin'."

It felt like liquid fire going down. Josh coughed and sputtered, trying to regain his breath. By the time he did, his comrade was guzzling freely.

"Running away?"

"No sir, I'm just on vacation."

"Sir?" The man cackled, revealing dingy teeth.

The liquor hit and Josh felt warmly numb. His insides quit shaking and he leaned back, exhausted.

"Thank you, sir. You saved my life."

"That depends. Just might've saved you for somethin' worse than you were running from." He coughed and spat on the floor then wiped his mouth against the arm of his ragged shirt. "What's your name, boy?"

"Joshua Smith."

"Wrong. First thing you got to learn on the run is don't leave no trail. Names are like Hansel with his breadcrumbs and no bird around to eat the tracks."

Josh nodded, feeling weariness overtake his bones. "I'd still like to know your name. I won't tell nobody else. Promise."

"Ain't got no name. Left it behind when I took off on my own vacation." He patted Josh's bruised arm, and Josh could smell body odor and the sweat his companion had worked up saving him. It was a comforting touch all the same. "You listen up good, boy. This train's headed for Chicago. Don't make a peep and you might make it. Big city makes it hard to find runaways. Want to tell me why you're running now?"

"My ma died when my sister was born, and then our daddy just died and Sarah got put in a home. They were going to tote me off to an orphan—"

"Don't know why you're running, don't care to know."

"Then why'd you ask?"

"I'm tryin' to teach you somethin', give you some schoolin' that's not in the books."

Josh considered that. Sounded like good advice. "Are you going to Chicago?" he asked hopefully.

"Me, I'm getting off at the next refuel stop."

"Can I come with you? I won't be any bother."

"Best you learn right now the only way to travel is alone. Now get you some rest and don't say no more. Me and the bottle want to get cozy."

Josh shut his eyes, meaning to pretend sleep. If he was careful, he could sneak out and follow his friend long enough to pick up more lessons before striking out on his own.

The liquor, the ordeal, the lull of the train's constant movement seduced him to sleep.

When Josh awoke the train was still moving but he was alone.

He looked around the emptiness, dark now since it was night. Rubbing his eyes, he tried to remember.

And then he wished he hadn't. He was glad his father wasn't here, glad no one could see the tears that big boys weren't supposed to cry.

Reaching into his pocket, he found a torn up Kleenex. And a five dollar bill. He knew it hadn't been there when he'd jumped the train. Remembering that protective hardness he'd summoned in Sarah's room, he drew on it again, replacing his tears with something gritty and determined.

When Josh Smith hit Chicago, he had five dollars, the clothes on his person, and a promise to keep. In less than a week he had a room in a deserted building where he'd fought the rats for space, a box he'd painted black, stuffed with clean rags and a can of saddle soap, plus a rickety chair he'd salvaged from an alley.

Joe, at a nearby greasy spoon, loaned him a spot on the corner and leftovers from the grill, in exchange for running errands and free shines.

Spotting a potential client, Josh wiped off the cracked vinyl seat and intercepted the man's path.

"Shine your shoes, mister? Fifty cents'll get you the full treatment. Spit polished and shiny as a new penny."

The man sat and Josh had his first customer. "You got a name, son?"

"Rand Slick," Josh said, quickening his buffing strokes.

As good a name as any for a man with no roots. A man in a boy's borrowed body who'd learned two rules from a bum:

Trust no one but if you do make damn sure they earned it.

And go the dark, endless road back home alone.

CHAPTER 1

Twenty Years Later - Las Vegas, 1995

"*M*ister?"

"What?"

"I said, shine your shoes, mister?"

Rand Slick blinked several times, willing the present to focus.

"Sorry, son, can't spare the time." He pulled out a platinum money clip and peeled off a Ben Franklin. "Grab a square meal but put the rest in your college fund. Best investment you'll ever make."

Rand hurried on, skirting a bum hugging a brown paper sack. He hated this sleazy quarter of Vegas. The atmosphere made him feel dirty, as though his bespoke suit and Allen Edmonds wing tips were molting, leaving him in rags and battered shoes. Nothing but his ongoing quest to find his sister Sarah could induce him to relive the bad old days of youth.

He entered a rundown building, his hopes lowering with each step on threadbare carpet. His sources had said this PI was good, but the seedy surroundings made him wonder.

He scanned the faded lettering on yellowed milk glass office doors until he stood in front of one that smelled of Windex. The black ink scored into clear beveled glass was carefully etched and looked new.

"Rachel Tinsdale, Private Investigator," he read. His flagging spirits climbed a notch when he opened the door and a tinkling wind chime announced his entry. The scent of potpourri and lemon oil masked the mustiness of age. The office was neat, the furniture second hand but warmly vintage. A big oak desk that belonged to a schoolroom from the 50's sported a mild litter of files, a tall plaid thermos bottle, a Route 66 coffee mug, and a bottle of bright red nail polish. The burnt orange vinyl chair behind the desk appeared to be vacant—until he saw it slightly bob.

"Have a seat and I'll be right with you."

The invitation came from under the desk. He frowned. Voices could be deceiving, but this one sounded, well, kittenish, like an ingénue from an old Elvis movie. Not a good sign. Quick reflexes and courage and sharp thinking were essential for the job he needed done. Maybe his sources were wrong.

His steps were muffled by a big, slightly threadbare oriental rug. Once he was positioned by the desk's side he got a view of flowing red hair, a slender back covered in white cotton, and what appeared to be a cute little tush bobbing on the edge of the orange vinyl. Presuming this was Ms. Tinsdale, her backside package was better than nice. While such credentials were important for his hiring purposes, even more imperative were skills he could trust in the face of danger.

Perfect opportunity. And seizing opportunity was, after all, his stock and trade.

"Don't move," he ordered in a low, menacing tone. "Stop what you're doing and just do as I say."

"Sure. As soon as I finish painting this last toenail."

Her safety was supposedly at risk and she was worried about painting her toes? He darted a glance at the red nail polish bottle beside the files on her desk. The top of the bottle was still on.

Just what the hell was she doing under the desk?

"Before you ransack the office you might as well know I've got ten bucks to my name," said the ingénue voice with the sweet tush to match. "Why don't you save yourself the bother of tearing the place up, and me the mess? Here's my purse." A large straw handbag with **ALOHA** emblazoned across the middle was shoved over the floor in his direction, the action making her rear bob a little higher while Rand's seasoned eyes narrowed appreciatively.

"Go ahead," she said. "Pick it up. The billfold's at the bottom and the money's stashed in the change compartment. But you'd better hurry because I've got an appointment any minute and you're liable to get caught."

Rand granted her credit for ingenuity as well as questionable taste in purses. She had his interest though, so, playing along, he stooped to pick up the bag.

How she did it he had no idea but Ms. Tinsdale was no longer under the desk. She sent the chair wheeling, knocked him down so his back hit wood, and had the barrel of a gun pointed in the middle of his face.

As for her face, he was too focused on the gun to note more than a glimpse of...*whew.*

"Okay punk, lock your arms over your head, roll over, and if you move so much as a hair I'll blow your head off."

"But—"

"No ifs, ands, or buts. If you're packing, I'm finding. Now once more since you seem a little dumb: Roll over. Arms over your head. Legs spread. Time for a little body search."

He should start talking and fast. Then again, having his body searched by Ms. Tinsdale had a certain appeal. To check out her investigative skills, of course.

Rand followed her orders.

Her free hand efficiently frisked his arms but when she glided it over his ribs and back, he could feel himself getting into this in a way that had nothing to do with business.

"I think you'd better stop," he said gruffly.

"Getting too close to something you don't want me to find?"

I'll say, he thought. Her hand was nearly patting his rear which was awfully close to an area that didn't care his primary interest in Ms. Tinsdale was in hiring her for other undercover purposes.

"Aren't you a tad overdressed for the occasion?" she scoffed. "No, don't tell me. You're a hood who likes to make a statement so you ripped off the threads." Agile fingers gripped one ankle, then the other, checking for a hidden weapon. "Nice socks. Cashmere?"

When she made a svelte glide over the back of his left thigh, he groaned.

"Ms. Tinsdale," he said raggedly, "Why don't you save us both some embarrassment and stop where you are?"

"How do you know my name?" She did stop unfortunately. Her palm rested near his crotch. "The door, of course. Ah-hah! Thought you could fool me, did you?"

She went for the other leg.

"Ms. Tinsdale!" he said urgently. "*Enough.* I'm Rand Slick. I'm here for our appointment to discuss a missing person."

"Rand Slick?" she exclaimed. "Ohmygosh!"

Cognizant of her quick scramble to offer him a hand up, Rand prudently kept his supine position—only for his gaze to collide with the most luminous green eyes he'd ever seen.

For a moment they stared at each other. His initial impression of *whew* became an outright *WOW*. Rachel Tinsdale wasn't merely attractive. She was...arresting. Interesting, in a *how could you ever forget a face like that?* sort of way. Creamy complexion with a light smattering of freckles over a delicate nose, rosebud lips, a sweet jawline punctuated by a dimple in her chin. But it was more than that and whatever more it was only heightened his awareness of a palpable tension suffusing the potpourri and lemon scented air.

"Think you could put the rod away?" he asked. "I have an aversion to being on the wrong side of a trigger."

As quickly as the connection had happened, she broke it. She strode a few feet to pick up her purse, returned the gun to it. As she did Rand was snared by the swish of long, vivid red hair, the sleek, poetic movement of her back, the exposure of slim ankle and nicely shaped calves that flowed up and under the sway of a vintage shirtdress, cinched at her waist. Shiny black pumps matched her belt; a red chiffon scarf tied at her neck and a wide tortoise shell headband completed her look. Nothing about her would qualify for predictable or familiar—and yet he had this strange sense of déjà vu. Maybe because she could have walked off the set of *Grease* singing "Look At Me, I'm Sandra Dee."

When she offered her hand again, this time he took it.

Her palm was dry but he caught a faint shake. Or maybe it came from him. Had to be a belated reaction to the gun nearly shoved up his nose.

With surprising strength, she helped him to his feet. Toe-to-toe, she came just to his chin. Hers notched up. For looking so delicate it sure had a stubborn set to it.

"Do you care to tell me what that little stick-up act was all about, Mr. Slick? I could've blown your head off."

"Sorry. I wanted to test your reflexes. Not a good move on my part I'm afraid."

She snorted her agreement then nodded to a wicker chair facing her desk. As they sat opposite each other she appeared composed, minus the light tapping of a pen to a file folder. His respect, and his hopes, climbed. He knew all about faking it till you made it, and Ms. Tinsdale was doing a helluva job. Not only that, she was one first-class frisker. He shifted in the chair, feeling an uncomfortable reminder.

"Tell me," she said. "Do you make it a habit to hit people out of left field? Or was this just a lapse into—"

"Stupidity?" He chuckled. "Sorry, I can be a bit unorthodox in my methods. But I get my answers and results one way or the other."

"As do I, Mr. Slick. Apology accepted." Tap. Tap. "So, were your answers/results satisfactory enough to get down to the business that brings you here?"

Rand raised an appreciative brow. "Where do you suggest we start?"

Minutes later, Rachel still felt like a bouncing ball in a roulette wheel that hadn't stopped spinning since the hunk in her office locked eyes with her on the floor. Rand Slick was *hot*. Like smokin'. With that swarthy olive skin and those glistening straight white teeth, just call him the big bad wolf in a "I got money, honey" suit and Gucci tie. He was handsome for sure, but there was nothing soft to balance out the stern planes of his face. His eyes were a deep, chocolate brown, the same shade as his executive cut hair. Great mouth. Nice jaw. Nothing weak about either.

Growing up in the PI business had netted her fine instincts on first impressions. Rand Slick had a polished exterior that hid some dangerously rough edges. He reminded her of Rocky Balboa—the kind of man who maintained an aura of the streets no matter how far he moved up in the world. Or maybe it was just those muscles of his that felt more brawler tough than work-out lean.

He pointed to the thin file that had arrived the day before via Fed Ex. "As I was saying, I didn't want to inundate you with too many details until we had a face-to-face, see if we had the right chemistry for a partnership and you had a genuine interest in taking on my case."

He was waiting for a response. She'd hated chemistry in high school, but there was chemistry and then there was *chemistry*. Like *ka-pow!* The tummy drop kind.

Chemistry aside, even if she was desperate for clients in her new practice, there was an underlying sense of desperation on his end that suggested Rand Slick had been turned down one too many times and she, with the ink barely dry on her license, was a last resort to take on his case.

Red flag.

"I'm certainly interested, Mr. Slick—"

"Rand. Call me Rand."

"Rand, then. And enough with the Ms. Tinsdale while we're at it. But I do have some concerns. It's not so much about what this itsy-bitsy file of yours says, but what it doesn't. Now just so we're clear, you have reason to believe that your sister was spotted at a local casino six months ago, and hasn't been seen since, correct?"

"Correct."

"And prior to that, just when was the last time that you personally saw, or spoke to, your sister?"

His engaging expression turned stony. Like she had intruded on a gravesite bearing a bomb instead of roses.

"That's private information I'm not quite ready to dispense."

"Ohhh...kay." But it wasn't. Rachel tried again. "When Harry Cline approached me about meeting with you, he said you've got some mutual business interests. I pressed him for some personal details about you. Interestingly, he didn't seem to know much. I'd like to know more about you. Rand."

"I didn't come here to discuss myself. Let's stick to any information you need regarding my sister."

Rachel didn't like his "back off" tone. She'd picked up on the rough edges, but she hadn't been prepared for them to emerge so abruptly. Whoever Rand Slick was, he definitely was not a man people messed with. Took a lot to unnerve her, but he did with his tense posture, a sharp but strangely distant stare.

Never let nobody know you're shook, she remembered her dad saying. *Look 'em in the eyeballs and even if your insides turn to mush don't back down.*

Rachel pushed back her shoulders, sat up straighter. Fortunately, the desk hid the foot she was shaking.

"In that case tell me everything you can about Sarah, no matter how unimportant it seems. Her habits, her hobbies, and especially the kind of people she hangs out with."

For a split second she glimpsed something vulnerable in his expression. The unexpected reaction caught her like a velvet upper-cut to the right before she'd recovered from the brass-knuckled sting from the left.

"She's seven years younger than me. That puts her at twenty-five. I know next to nothing about her habits or what she does for kicks. The people she hangs out with have been as elusive as herself."

"Do you have a picture?"

Again, a flash of unguarded emotion—then just as quickly, gone. He reached inside his suit coat pocket and handed her a faded snapshot. He looked away while she studied it.

Rachel's heart softened on a lurch. There was a story in this picture. A very sad story. It wasn't so much the image of Rand Slick as a young boy hugging a little girl who stared up at him adoringly. It was the creased texture of glossy paper, the edges rubbed smooth from years of constant touching.

She struggled to appear unaffected. This was not a person who liked to expose himself and any sympathy from her would be deflected. Besides, there was the cardinal rule: A PI must *never* get emotionally involved in a case. It was unprofessional. It clouded your judgement. *Snake eyes.*

"Nothing more recent?"

"We were separated shortly after this picture was taken," was his answer. "She was five."

He was holding out. *Why?* "How did you come to be separated?"

"It doesn't matter. What does is that I've been tracking her for years and run into one dead end after another. The family she was living with died when their house caught fire."

"She got out?"

"They lived in the country but I understand from the closest neighbors she ran off a year earlier with a drifter who was passing through. She was a senior in high school."

"But you'd recognize her if you saw her?"

"Absolutely."

"Even though you haven't seen her since she was five."

"I..."

He winced. *Got him.* "Go on."

"I...yes, I did have occasion to see her after we were separated. Twice. Once when she was ten and then at fourteen. And I did recognize her. A brother knows his sister no matter how many years pass."

"Did you talk to her on either or both occasions?"

"No."

"Why not?"

"Because there were too many people around and I—" He passed a hand over his eyes, concealing whatever emotion he didn't want her to see. "It was an unusual situation. Don't ask me to explain. Please."

The last word seemed hard for him to get out, as though he was requesting a personal favor and asking favors didn't come easy. She had also noticed that while he kept his voice even there was an undercurrent of something old and raw, like a scab that had been picked at too often to properly heal.

Obviously more than a flesh wound. Best to pick delicately while appearing to respect his need for privacy.

Rachel extended the photo. Their hands touched. They came to an understanding with that touch. She just might care. He needed her to care enough to share his search.

They shared more. A distinct but disturbing current was passing from him to her. It was achingly personal and something she couldn't acknowledge with a client. Especially not a dark charmer that seemed about as predictable as a coin toss.

"There's more." He pocketed the snapshot. "You might as well know five different detectives have worked on this case."

"And where are they now?"

"Well paid and off the job I'm here to see you about."

"Any chance those well paid detectives handed over more than what I've got here?" Rachel arched a brow at the thin stack of pages on her desk.

"As I said, I didn't want to overwhelm you with too much, too soon. I have a thick file you're welcome to—along with some additional pictures—if we can come to terms first."

She wanted to tell him that's not how it worked. That he needed to cough up the goods before she decided whether or not they could come to terms. But this guy. He wasn't the usual customer.

"Tell you what, Rand. Since you're not ready to hand over the master file, and I'm working with a lot of blank space between here"—she pointed the pen from the folder to him—"and there, why don't you fill me in with a few more details while I take notes?" Flipping open a spiral notebook she'd bought just for this meeting, Rachel put pen to paper. "Do you know what happened after Sarah ran off?"

"Not much except that she kept moving."

"Do you know why she ran away to begin with? Could it have anything to do with why she stayed on the move?"

"Beats me. The family she was with seemed pretty solid. Who knows? Maybe it was just a crazy whim or an idea she picked up from…a bad influence." He cleared his throat and from beneath her lashes she could see him shifting as though the chair was a bun warmer and he wanted out from the toasty heat. "Anyway, I got pretty close several times, but either she had wanderlust or she was on the run."

"Any guess why?"

"My sources indicate the man she ran off with had some shady connections."

"Were your sources reliable?"

"They were shady enough themselves to make the connection."

Her pen stopped in mid-scratch. "Back up a minute. Are you telling me you're connected, and I don't mean with AT&T?"

As he raked a hand through his dark back-brushed hair, light filtered through flecks of silver. How much of his quest had put them there, she wondered? Didn't matter. Even if she sympathized with him, no way was she getting mixed up with the wrong crowd. Her reputation was more important than getting kicked out of this office because she couldn't pay the rent…or wasn't sure how she was going to pay for a transmission job on the '64 Mercury Comet she'd inherited from her dad…along with a pile of Daddy's IOU's…

"Look," Rand said, sighing. "I'm clean. I have no faith in the system and I do know some people outside it who've gotten me information that money can't buy. I don't set myself up to owe favors, only to collect. Relax. Whatever my connections, they're not who I am."

Rachel tapped the pen against the paper and studied him intently. Roll the dice.

"And just who are you, Mr. Slick?"

His jaw tightened; a muscle ticked in his cheek. He got up. Leaned over the desk. Any vulnerability she had sensed in him before was snuffed out by a towering man with a face of granite who was making her feel like Fay Wray squirming in King Kong's grip.

"Since you seem as concerned with my background as you are with this case I'll give you a little bio and then we'll drop it. What do you want to know? The ID I can't give for my sister?"

Don't back down. If you do, he's out of here. You keep hitting a nerve and now he's turning the tables. Again.

Rachel swallowed hard. "I like to know how my clients tick. If I'm risking my hide, you can't blame me for that."

His expression said that he could and he did.

"Okay, we'll start with the fact that I find pen tapping grating." He whipped the pen from her hand and tossed it to the desk. "As for habits, I brush my teeth two times a day and shower every morning. I drink moderately—Macallan 20 Year Scotch preferred —avoid emotional entanglements and practice safe sex. I'm a workaholic who enjoys an occasional game of racquetball or poker. I can't stand to lose and it's rare that I do. As for palling around, I prefer to fly solo." He smiled and she was reminded of a barracuda contemplating lunch.

His turnaround bothered her as much as the thought that being devoured by Rand Slick had a certain frightful appeal. Maybe Fay Wray secretly wanted to cuddle with King Kong, too.

"Now," he continued smoothly, "since you know more about me than most, it's your turn. I have some things I want to know about you. Rachel."

"What…what do you want to know?"

"Everything, actually. But for now I'll stick with some important specifics. Do you like to visit faraway places? Could you possibly endure being stripped in public? And by some miracle, is your virginity somewhat intact? If the answer is no to any or all, can you fake the first two if I make it worth your while?"

"What?"

"You heard me." He gripped her wrist and she wondered if he

could feel her pulse racing from the contact. His touch was compelling even as it sent off a shrilling alarm. "I need more than just another detective. I need a woman with guts and looks. You've got both. But they won't do me any good unless you're willing to stand on an auction block and go up for sale."

"You've got to be kidding."

"No. I'm not. Time is of the essence, so I'll cut to the chase: Not only do I need your skills, I need your body." His gaze raked an incisive path from her head to her breasts. The electric reaction triggered a protective cross of her free arm over her chest. "Good," he said, "The more innocent you appear, the better. If you've got the courage, I've got the in."

"What *are* you talking about?"

"The real reason for this meeting." He fixed her with a level stare. "I want to buy you."

Funny, he didn't look nuts. Jack the Ripper probably hadn't either.

Her wisest move would be to humor him until she could buzz security...only there wasn't any security in the building. *Dammit.*

"Of course," she said, forcing a smile and wondering if she could somehow retrieve the gun from her purse. "Did you have a payment schedule in mind?"

"You can name your price and quit fumbling for your gun. Hear me out and I'll leave if you don't want to cut the deal."

"I think you'd better get to it."

"I tracked my sister down after she was last seen here in Vegas, but I can't get to her without a special ticket." He leaned closer to Rachel's face. His breath was warm and she inhaled the subtle fragrance of bay and night spice. "Three words," he said in a low, uninflected voice. *"White. Slave. Trade."*

CHAPTER 2

"*D*id you just say White Slave Trade?"

Damn, Rand thought. He'd let his urgency blind his good sense. Hadn't he been turned down enough times without scaring this one off before she gave him half a chance?

Rand released her wrist, all too aware that her skin was baby soft and disturbingly pleasant to the touch. He didn't do a lot of touching, at least not the kind that came with any real emotional attachment. Sidecar bums and mean streets were good teachers. So were lonely socialite mentors with absent husbands. He wasn't particularly proud of all his educational tools, but he hadn't gotten this far by letting any of them go to waste.

"My apologies." His smile was appropriately apologetic, and a small part of him actually meant it. "You were asking all the right questions and if I came on a little too strong—"

"*If?*" Her glare was punctuated by a shake of her wrist.

He could apologize again. Apologize ten thousand times. But time was precious and if he couldn't gain her ear and her sympathy before day's end, he had to move on. No choice.

"I'll pay generously for the rest of your day. No strings, just a chance for you to hear me out."

Rand produced his money clip to back up his entreaty.

She was silent, probably weighing whether to take him seriously or question his mental stability. He caught her glancing in the direction of an appointment book. She opened it then shut it quickly, but not quickly enough. Rand looked away, appearing not to have seen a blank page, except for his name scribbled in.

"My fee is seventy dollars an hour."

Hmm. Chances were she had just increased her going rate. He liked that. The woman knew how to work a situation to her advantage.

"Why don't we make it an even thousand for the rest of the day?" Rand shelled out the cash and laid it on her closed appointment book. "I'd like to compensate for interfering with your schedule."

She looked from the neat stack of bills to him, a startled expression animating her face before she quickly disguised it.

"Well," she said slowly, appearing to debate. "I suppose I could break free since this seems to be urgent."

"It is. And if you don't mind moving this meeting elsewhere, would you be agreeable to an early lunch? I didn't have breakfast and I'm hungry. Another little fact about me: When I'm hungry, I tend to get cranky. So maybe you'll let me prove I can be a lot nicer with breadsticks on a table than I am with a pen on a desk." He angled his gaze at the tossed pen in question, grimaced. "Sorry about that."

She nodded her acceptance of his second apology for the day. He so hated to eat crow that he'd rather chug curdled milk. But when she picked up the stack of bills, frilled them—and then split his stack of green in half…

"Five hundred will do it—but I'll let you buy lunch."

Rand hesitated before reluctantly accepting her offering. This was not familiar territory. He had learned that money talked the most powerful, universal language in existence, but Rachel Tinsdale had just let him know that even if she accepted his case, he didn't have enough money in the world to buy her.

～

Rachel couldn't believe it. *Five hundred smackers!* She should have taken it all, obviously he could afford it, but her dad had taught her that greed came with a price. *It's just like a gold digger marrying for money, and earning every penny,* he'd told her. *Money is a good servant and a cruel master, so you be sure you marry for love. And don't forget that other thing I told you about men and cows.*

Her dad was Old School; he'd raised her on values like "Why buy a cow when you can get free milk?" which put him on a par with an evangelist preaching chastity in Sin City. Much as she missed her daddy, good thing he wasn't here. Rand Slick's keister would have already hit the sidewalk, maybe even taking a short cut out the window. Head first.

While she tucked his file and notebook into her oversized handbag that doubled as a briefcase, Rachel was all too aware of those dark eyes studying her every move and making her feel like a pithed frog under a microscope. *Chemistry* for sure. It was throwing her equilibrium off, not to mention getting her sidetracked by the way he was waiting, shoving his hands into his pockets so that his shirt strained and so did the fly of his pants.

Had she really just checked out his crotch?

"Hungry for anything in particular?"

Boy, was that a loaded bazooka. Rachel took a deep breath, kept her eyes on the door they were heading for, and suggested, "Nate's is just around the corner. Best greasy spoon in town if you don't mind a little wait."

"I'm sure it's, um, worth any wait, but if you don't mind I'd prefer someplace we could have a private conversation. I'm happy to drive, unless you'd rather do the driving."

Her car was in the transmission shop, but she didn't want to tip her strapped hand. When she hesitated, he offered, "Or would you rather take a taxi? I understand if you're uncomfortable getting into a car alone with me."

She was uncomfortable, but it came from the proximity of their bodies as they stood outside her office door while she finally latched onto the keys swimming low tide of ALOHA. Laps of energy that felt like radio waves riding the air tuned in on the fine hair prickling the back of her neck.

Rachel did her best to ignore it. He'd paid in advance and the least she could do was show some good faith.

"Starting now we're on your time, Rand. My office is officially closed for the day. You drive."

He smiled, seemingly pleased, but the quirk of his lips only managed to make her awkward and she cursed softly when the keys slipped from her grasp, clattered to the floor.

"I'll get them," he said.

They almost knocked heads. Their hands connected at the keys. For breathless seconds she couldn't move. Meaning to laugh the accident off and pretend there wasn't something so physically startling in the contact that it snuffed out her remaining composure, she slowly raised her face.

His breath was on her. There was a dark room behind his eyes, one that was as unchaste and ominous as it was lush with invitation. Leather and lace. Black velvet and white silk. Haunting. Erotic. Welcome to the Hotel California.

Rachel blinked, trying to get her balance. What was she doing? Decorating his bedroom and checking out his lighting scheme? Rand was way out of her range of experience and this was a professional meeting, even if her circus act stomach insisted it was more.

She took an unsteady breath and managed a faint smile.

"Not a smooth move, huh?"

"I like the way you move."

Rachel quickly raised up and shoved the key in. *Damn, why couldn't she get it to lock?* She was jiggling it and silently swearing like crazy when he caught her hand. Her breathing was not normal. Nothing had seemed normal since he'd walked through the stupid door she couldn't get locked.

"Let me." His hand glided over hers, working the key. It clicked. For several seconds they remained still, but then he broke the contact and Rachel exhaled the breath she'd been holding.

"Thanks," she said to fill up the taut silence. "That's a testy door. It takes a special touch to get it to cooperate."

"Seems your door and I have a lot in common." He grinned devilishly and Rachel felt like she'd just tripped over something.

She glanced down, almost expecting to see her heart, along with her tummy-drop stomach, playing chase on the floor.

When they reached his car—and wouldn't you just know it was a Mercedes—he opened the passenger door like they were on a date instead of out for a business lunch. It bothered her that it didn't bother her. She liked the way he lifted an edge of her skirt that trailed the ground after she slid her buns over some really nice leather that still had that new car smell; how he draped the vintage fabric over her lap and instructed, "Buckle up. I've got a vested interest in keeping you safe."

As the door shut she knew she didn't feel safe at all. She felt like she was sneaking out past curfew to hook up with the kind of fast boy her father had warned her to steer clear of.

She watched how he strode around the car, got in; even the way he pulled out and navigated traffic, it all smacked of purpose. Ditto for the CD he slid into the car's player while he slid her a smile that matched his selection. Water music: dipping flute notes, the rippling cascade of a sitar. Winding. Tantalizing. Sensual.

"Do you like it?" he asked casually, when clearly there was nothing casual about this car or his choice in music. All that was missing were some belly dancers and an opium den.

"It's very exotic."

"Any other impressions? Close your eyes and tell me what you see."

The low, mesmerizing tone of his voice blended into the hypnotic lull of the clear, undulating notes. She closed her eyes and for a moment was transported to a faraway world.

"I see...camels, white tents and flowing robes, sand and palms." She laughed softly. "A hookah on a carved teak table next to a brass lamp that might belong to Aladdin. Big plump pillows on Persian rugs. It's a scene from the *Arabian Nights*."

"And do you smell anything?"

"Sandalwood, incense, and..." *Bay and night spice*. Rachel's eyes snapped open. Quickly she added, "My dad always did say I had a vivid imagination. I get carried away with it sometimes."

Rand stopped the car and she vaguely noted that they were parked in front of an exclusive establishment. The exotic setting was still with her, catching her up in the tendrils of music which continued to play. Rand was studying her closely, not making his expected move to get out. And here she was, all but mooning over a potential client, pretending they were sharing the sense-thick scenario she had spun.

Rachel went for the door.

"Wait." He caught her hand in mid-reach of the handle. There was something distinctly intimate in the gesture. "Your imagination's more than vivid, Rachel. It's very close to reality. Have you ever heard of a small Eastern country by the name of Zebedique?"

"No," she said quietly, acutely aware he didn't release her hand. Could he feel her small shake, the one that hummed to a sweet vibration through her nervous system?

"I'd like to tell you a little about Zebedique," he went on. "It's very similar to the place you described. Rich, excessive, you could even say hedonistic. I own a house there. Quite a bit different from my place in New York."

"I don't guess this Zebedique property is a vacation getaway from the city that never sleeps?" Like Vegas ever called it a night. As for what he was doing in Vegas when New York was home…his sister, of course. The sister she'd almost forgotten about. Rachel winced, upset with herself. This was no way to start out her new practice.

"Zebedique is the last place I would take a vacation. I own property there for a reason."

"Sarah."

He nodded. "Yes. It's highly segregated—which is why I need a woman, a frankly unique woman, who's resourceful and not afraid to pose as my…well, someone who has access to areas where only women are allowed."

He was watching her closely, choosing his words carefully, obviously not wanting to scare her off. No need, she thought, she was scaring herself enough.

"Go on, Rand. You're paying me to listen. I'm all ears." She felt a single fingertip glaze over the moisture of her palm, making her nerve ends leapfrog then collide as they jumped. She needed to get her hand back. Only…

What was happening to her felt dangerous. It felt *delicious.*

She let him keep her hand, sweaty palm and all.

"Okay, I'll be blunt. I have a plan that can get you in, as, shall we say, a desirable acquisition. No one would buy you but me and once I did no one else would dare touch you. There are harsh penalties for trying to encroach on another man's territory, and you'd be considered my personal property."

"Your…personal…property."

"Yes. Once the transaction is made, it's up to the owner's discretion as to how they wish to utilize their, ah, property."

"I don't suppose the women being acquired are there to clean houses?"

"No," he confirmed. "They're being sold for sexual purposes to the men who buy them. These aren't just any men, Rachel. We're talking about extraordinarily wealthy and powerful men from around the world with the means to protect their identities. I understand that virgins go for a premium, given supply, and American women are especially in demand because the slavers are afraid to risk many abductions. The ones they do abduct seem to be without family to miss them."

"And meanwhile Sarah has no idea she has a brother shadowing her back." Rachel shook her head. "How terrible for her to think that she has no hope."

"It is terrible and I try not to think it. I need you, Rachel. I realize this is a serious decision that can't be made on a moment's notice, but time is precious. All I can promise is that if you agree, once we're there and the transaction made, I will protect you." Something troubled, even haunted, was in the gaze he didn't try to hide or disguise this time. "It's important to keep promises. Hope-fully the one I made to Sarah a long time ago isn't coming too late."

It was the most personal admission he had freely offered thus far—and it told her more about him than it did about Sarah. Rand Slick, Promise Keeper. As for what promise he had made, she didn't sense he was quite ready to give that up so freely.

"About this house of yours in Zebedique?" she ventured.

"Where we'd live—the two of us. We'd have to give the appear-ance of our expected roles." He smiled. Sort of. "You can act, can't you Rachel? It wouldn't be unpleasant. The place has quite a lay out. I have an office already set up, there's a pool, a sauna, servants around to do the cooking and cleaning. You'd have your very own handmaid. I understand she used to be a masseuse. Just think, in your off time you could get back rubs."

If she was getting massages in her off time, Rachel had to

wonder just what he had in mind when she was on the clock. "About our roles. What would they entail?"

Rand released her hand, reached for his door. When she followed suit, he caught her wrist again.

"For one thing it would mean I act like the sultan of the palace while you pretend to stroke my ego. Just in case we can strike a deal, how about a little practice? You stay put and I'll come around to get you. Then once we're in the restaurant I'll order for us both and you look like you're hanging onto my every word when I bore you silly talking about my arbitrage business."

"Do I have to laugh if you tell a bad joke?"

"I understand all good concubines do."

"Concu—"

His door shut. *Concubine!* Hadn't that word gone out with the Old Testament? The CD shut off and Rachel was left with the uneasy impression that the music and the word went together strangely well.

CHAPTER 3

*T*hey extended their early lunch into an early Happy Hour. Rand topped off their champagne flutes while Rachel excused herself to the lady's room. He watched the alluring combination of slender ankles, shapely legs and hourglass curves that swayed in tandem with her gliding stride.

He liked her walk. It had attitude.

There was a lot about her that he liked. Maybe a bit too much. He'd have to be careful or she might slip under his skin, which was more than he could say for the string of women and affairs that had comprised what he supposed was a personal life.

Rand sipped his champagne, mentally toasting his good fortune. If he was going to buy a woman, Rachel Tinsdale was definitely the one he wanted to own. He hadn't gotten her to agree yet, but he would.

If exposing himself enough to evoke her compassion and playing on the surprising physical tug between them didn't work, money would do the trick. In his experience, it always did. Then again, Rachel didn't seem to act on that modus operandi. He had five big ones back in his pocket to prove it. For some reason that bothered him. Maybe because it made him feel devalued, reminded him of something he'd lost along the way: emotions he couldn't afford and qualities that didn't have a price tag.

"Now where were we?" Rachel smiled and he felt an unfamiliar throb penetrate his senses. Before she could reseat herself he got up and helped push in her chair. She was lighter than air, and when she laughed softly at the gesture it felt like effervescent bubbles seeping into his pores. Natural. Wholesome. Lush.

Whew.

He saluted her with his glass and she hit him with a hearty burst of laughter before he'd recuperated from the after effects of her full lipped grin.

"What's so funny? I haven't even told you a bad joke yet."

"I just thought of this silly toast my dad used to say." She giggled and sipped at her champagne. When she looked over the rim her eyes sparkled. Rand was startled to feel something jolt him dead-center like a bulls-eye zap into a runaway target that thought it would never get hit.

"Now I'm curious." *And nursing a raging hard-on that's got nothing and everything to do with getting you to agree to share sleeping space with me.* "You were going to tell me about your dad and how you grew up anyway, so why don't we start with his toast?"

"I couldn't possibly say it in here."

"Why not?"

"Because this place is so classy."

She glanced around and patted her lips with the linen napkin to hide the giggle she couldn't quite control. He'd noticed the way she had emulated his choice of fork or knife during the meal. Discreetly, with a PI's ability to play a charade, but he'd deliberately used an incorrect one and she'd mirrored the action.

It reminded him of when he'd spent many a hard earned dollar to order an iceberg wedge or a cup of Vichyssoise in ritzy places like this. Watching. Assimilating. Mimicking the manners of the elite then returning to his hole in the wall to wolf down a substandard pizza or hotdogs with a can of pork and beans.

No, she didn't fit here any better than he did and it gave him a sense of something shared. Such a strange feeling, but strangely pleasant.

"Look, Rachel, you're classier than that high-brow bitching at her husband at the next table and I'm a paying customer. I'd say that gives us the right to toast however we damn well please." Rand lifted his glass. "C'mon, indulge me. Then you can indulge me some more and tell me about your dad."

She shrugged. "We still have a lot to discuss. You're sure this is how you want to spend your time?"

"We will. I am. And let's hear it. Sultan's decree."

"In that case, touch your glass to your nose."

Rand did as instructed, though his attention was on the cute way Rachel's nose turned up and crinkled as the tiny bubbles tickled it. The light sprinkling of freckles across the delicate bridge only seemed to emphasize the fact she was still a baby compared to him, a mere twenty-three, but man oh man just stick a quarter in him now and he'd start playing *Young Girl*.

"Next you have to growl." She demonstrated with a little Tony the Tiger "grrr" that he picked up with more mature overtones. His lids dipped to half-mast and hers opened wide.

"Uh, that's—that's very good, Rand. A little ferocious, but definitely into the spirit. Kind of."

"Maybe you should show me again," he suggested, pulling his chair closer to hers. Leaning in, he inhaled her unique scent that was somehow familiar but elusive. *What was she wearing, where had he smelled it before?* No clue. All he knew was that money smelled good but Rachel made money smell like dirt. "Growl for me. Soft but deep in your throat."

She hesitated, then he heard a sweet undulation sift into a kitten-like purr.

"Purr-fect," he whispered.

She quickly reached for her champagne. Rand intercepted the movement and put the glass to her lips, raising it slightly so that a trickle escaped the side of her take-me-now mouth.

"Rand," she said in a strangled voice. "Rand, those people are watching us."

"Let them. Now let's finish your dad's toast and give them something to talk about besides what they were arguing over."

"But it's for a noisy bar or a party with friends."

"Then let's be friends and have our own private party." Friends. He'd like that with her, he realized. And then he found himself exposing his truer colors, feeling his mouth forming the words while his ears could scarce believe he was lowering the guard that was his constant companion. "Pretentiousness doesn't score many points with me, Rachel, so don't ask me why I picked this place out. Honestly, I'm more at home in a corner bar than hobnobbing with the likes of our fellow diners. Now let's do this."

"Rocky," she whispered. He quirked a brow in question and she claimed her glass. "Okay, here goes: Look Out Mouth." His gaze settled on her lips. She wet them and he managed not to try for a taste of her little pink tongue. "Look Out Gums. Open up throat. Here it comes!"

Rand released a belly deep laugh. Real laughter in his life was a rare gift. And so was this feeling he couldn't quite describe—like he wanted to pull her out of the rain and into a phone booth where she couldn't escape. And neither could he.

"Lady, you are dynamite."

As Rachel laughed along with him she was fully aware that if anything was getting blown away it was her usually good senses, and she really needed to get this meeting back on track.

"Honestly, Rand, I'm a lot closer to a bowl of snap-crackle-pop."

"Says who? You? Or some significant other I'd like to know about if there's one hanging around."

Rachel hesitated as his eyes narrowed on her. Rand Slick wasn't someone to toy with. If she was smart she'd tell him she was heavily involved with someone who didn't exist.

"No significant other."

"Excellent. Now let's get back to this father of yours. Something tells me he taught you more than a toast and how to frisk a hood making a statement."

Rachel laughed self-consciously, reminded of their hands-on intro. Those muscles of his were...better not to remember. Better to think about all that her father had taught her, the core values and expectations he had instilled—important things like, "keep your britches up and don't let me down." It was a brand of wisdom that didn't have a mother's touch, but never had she doubted that Joe Tinsdale loved her as much as any child could ever be loved and he had done his best to bring her up right without a birth mother in sight.

"Daddy raised me. His PI buddies helped raise me, too, so even after Daddy didn't make it after a heart attack last year, I wasn't left all alone. I don't know much about my mother. Daddy said she died before I was old enough to remember much about her. For some reason he didn't have any pictures."

"Do you believe what he told you?"

No one had asked her that before. It should feel intrusive, but it didn't. Finally. A chance to say aloud what she'd secretly suspected for years.

"No," she confessed. "I think my mother was a call girl and my daddy stepped up to the plate, even if he wasn't sure I was his, before she took off."

Rand sat back, stroked his chin. With a jaw line like that he should be doing ads for Gillette. And why was she just noticing what great ears he had, too? Probably because she hadn't been able to take her eyes off everything else.

"Did your father have red hair?"

"No."

"Green eyes?"

Rachel shook her head.

"Then whoever your mother was gets major points for passing along some incredibly gorgeous genes despite any of her character flaws."

Rachel smiled, greatly pleased by his compliment. She touched her hair, then stroked her fingers through it while her eyes did some quick blinking. Suddenly she realized what she was doing. Preening! She was preening for him and wishing he was doing the touching instead of her. Rachel jerked her hand away.

"Anyway, Daddy did the best he knew how bringing me up. He signed me onto a softball team when I was six and taught me to throw a punch when the boys said I pitched like a girl."

"He sounds like the kind of father who might've run some of those boys off once you were older."

"I'll say. He told me boys had one thing on their minds and he should know since he was one of them. He had this test for judging them. Handshakes. Said you could tell a lot about a man by the way he shook hands. A limp handshake? Wimp. A firm handshake meant guts."

As he chuckled, Rand loosened his tie—a dark indigo Italian number, not one of her dad's paisleys or plaids. She couldn't take her eyes off the way he worked the silk to relax, then fingered the top button of his crisp white dress shirt to loosen the collar. The initials *RS* were discreetly embroidered on his cuff. It slightly rose as he stretched, revealing silky dark hair and a Rolex on his wrist. Her gaze slid to his chest. Without his suit coat on she could discern the width and proportions of his musculature. Again she was reminded of a street tough with a smooth veneer. Rocky.

Slamming his punches into a side of beef. The underdog coming out on top, compensating for life's short-comings with grit and character. She hadn't tested his handshake but she didn't doubt for a second that Rand Slick had guts and then some.

"I can understand his wanting to be protective," said the man who reeked of money, looked like a movie star, and could sell tickets just to watch him shave. "It's something I've felt in the past. The distant past." His expression let her know he hadn't missed where she'd been looking. "So. Besides playing ball, throwing punches, and screening your dates' handshakes, what else did you pick up from your dad?"

"Target shooting. Hanging around his office, learning the business. Sitting in on poker games with him and the boys while they drank whiskey, smoked cigars, swapped jokes. I learned a lot of bad words that I wasn't allowed to say."

Rand tapped a finger to his lips. She wished he wouldn't do that. It drew too much attention to his much too kissable mouth, and she'd bet dollars to doughnuts that he sure knew how to use it.

"I can imagine it must have been hard at times growing up like that. Setting you apart from other kids your age." He hesitated, but then she felt his hand cover hers. "I know what that's like."

A small silence fell between them, one that was easy but not. She felt a sense of sharing a common bond—only for the waiter to break into their tentative liaison with the discreet presentation of their bill.

As they walked to the car, Rand kept his hand at the small of her back. The light touch sparked a tingle at the base of her spine then shot in opposing directions, feeling like the rays that shimmered from a now setting sun. Just how long had they been in there? Long enough that lunch had slid into champagne and what Rand called tapas. And in all that time, they'd hardly discussed anything about Sarah or his case.

Some PI she was. Her conduct in the restaurant had been

anything but professional and her thoughts had been even less. She should feel miserable about it. She didn't. But that still did not change the fact that he had a case to be investigated and an invested interest in getting her signed up. She thought his interest in her as a person was genuine, but in the end this was about him and his sister, not her. And she couldn't discount the possibility of being subtly manipulated for his personal purposes. If so, it didn't make him a bad guy. That's just the way the world worked when people got squeezed into a corner and had to figure a way out.

"You didn't tell me about how you grew up. Or how you came to lose Sarah."

For a fleeting moment something poignant softened Rand's features. But then he erased it. She watched Rocky transform into a renovated skyscraper, all the cracks and damage disguised by plaster patches, fresh coats of paint and tightly sealed windows. One-way windows. The kind designed to look out but deflecting the view of anyone trying to look in.

Funny thing about windows, she thought. They had a way of getting broken or left open. Glass was fragile and accidents did happen.

"I lost Sarah to fate, Rachel. As for growing up, let's just say I had to figure out a lot of things at an early age."

"Anything else you're willing to tell me?"

"I can tell you that arbitrage is a risky business with big returns if you've got a knack for juggling two things at the same time. I buy and sell securities simultaneously when I detect a discrepancy in the going price. The way I operate is by getting rid of what I buy almost before I acquire it. In rare cases I hang onto something for myself. If you're good, and I am, big profits are reaped. If you screw up, and that's easy to do, it's immediate death."

She frowned, disappointed.

"You think I told you nothing, don't you?"

"You explained your line of business but left out much of personal importance."

"Read between the lines, Rachel. After all, you're a PI. You should be good at this." He waved her into the car and she got in. Rand leaned close, bay and night spice evoking water music images. For a moment she wondered wildly if he might try to kiss her. "While I drive you can think me over. Who knows? Maybe you'll figure me out, which is more than anyone else has ever pulled off."

"I don't guess you're feeling generous enough to spare a hint or two?"

His lips thinned, and then slowly shifted to a sly smile. "Think of me as a Rubik's Cube. But even if you solve it, the colors won't quite line up because a few slots are missing. The hinges are stubborn too. Comes from some jagged edges on the inside that've been there too long to give from their old groove."

As he drove, Rachel stole glances at his profile while she puzzled the maze. Missing: Sarah. But what else? And what had caused the jagged edges Rand seemed more comfortable with than the risk of self-exposure?

The music hovered between them, slipping into the crevices of her mind and playing tricks on reality. She could see him in another time, another place, a great autonomous ruler who was a mystery to all...except for a woman who was his greatest pleasure by day, his secret keeper in the deep of the night. She saw her draped in gossamer, her skin pale against his hands as he swept the thin barrier aside and her gown pooled to the floor.

Rachel couldn't see her face. Yet she couldn't deny that more than anything, she wanted the woman to be her.

CHAPTER 4

*R*and leaned back into the cushions of Rachel's old couch. It had been a long five days since he'd had to cut their meeting short and rush back to New York to straighten out a potential mess on a high-stakes acquisition.

He'd never thought he would be champing at the bit to make another trip to Vegas. He hadn't expected himself to find excuses to call just so he could hear her voice. He was deeply attracted to the sound of it. The kittenish freshness of her tone; that breathless little catch that made him feel like the earth had changed the rules of gravity and he was moonwalking the New York concrete.

In a matter of days he had logged a solid ten hours on the phone with Rachel.

He hated to talk on the phone. Time was money. His longest conversations were typically minutes at best. I.E. "Here's the deal, take it or leave it…Oh, you don't like my terms? Fine. When you come crawling back, the deal's ten percent less."

He could get mean. He could get ugly. It was easy because he could detach. Rachel was messing with that. She could be beneficial to him personally but bad for business.

Staring at her bent head while she studied Sarah's file across from him, Rand thought of how he'd all but run to Rachel's front door tonight, eager, and yet certain he was imagining the whole crazy thing. And then he wasn't certain of anything, not even his name because she'd knocked the supports out from under him with a single dazzling smile.

Whump! He'd felt the ground tilt while a soft, tingling blow clobbered him right between the eyes. He didn't know what the hell hit him while he stood there speechless, wondering how the ingénue in a white vintage dress had transformed into a young Ann Margret, poured into a pair of little black pencil pants, an off the shoulder pink sweater that hugged her in all the right places, and penny loafers with real copper coins shining from the middle. Her stop traffic hair was swept up into a ponytail with an old scarf playing hide-and-seek through a riot of red tendrils.

She smelled even better than he remembered—a whisper of nostalgia wrapped in temptation. It was like inhaling a controlled substance designed to drive a man absolutely out of his mind.

Rachel suddenly looked up.

"You're staring at me."

"Caught me. Want me to stop?"

"No—I mean, yes. You make it hard to concentrate."

"Do I? Sorry," he lied, then managed a half truth. "I'm trying to judge your reaction to what you're reading." He leaned over and tapped a well-thumbed page. "I see you've gotten to the heart of the matter."

"The last investigator you hired did a good job. Several slavers operating under a single umbrella and shipping to one port. Zebedique." She tossed several photographs from the file onto the coffee table between them. "These newer pictures of Sarah say a lot. At least one can only assume it's her underneath enough layers of sackcloth to bake a cake."

"That's her. The men I hired to keep Sarah under surveillance confirmed it. I didn't show you these particular photos until now since I felt they were more graphic than if she'd been wearing nothing. Maybe you can understand why I held out on you."

"I do, and it was probably a smart move on your part. Even knowing what I do now I can hardly believe what I'm looking at. It's another world and not one I'd ever want to be in. Imagine, living without the freedom to walk alone or even choose how you want to dress." Rachel studied the pictures a moment longer before replacing them in the file. She shook her head, snorted her disgust. "This is a very nasty business, Rand. It needs to be exposed."

"As soon as I've got Sarah. Any tip off to the authorities before then would implicate the casino manager that's raking in his dirty pay-offs. Go after him, he squeals on his crooked buddies, and any chance of me getting to Sarah before the alarms start sounding is dead. I am *not* taking that chance."

"But this has been going on too long. Sarah disappeared months ago and who knows how many women have been abducted since? Surely there's another way besides the one we've discussed."

"Rachel, trust me, I've exhausted every other angle. I've kept round the clock surveillance in Zebedique since I traced Sarah there. I've made two trips and have nothing to show for it except for some real estate and being utterly convinced she's too heavily guarded to make a successful snatch. Unless you can come up with a better idea, I see no other way but to make the connection at the bathhouse she's taken to on Fridays."

"Women only, right?"

"That's right. Massages, whirlpools, saunas. I understand from one of the servants I hired—the masseuse that would be your guard—that the concubines are left unattended in the sauna."

"They're not afraid their prisoners might escape?"

"Hardly. Not when they're naked and have to be covered from head to toe just to walk down the street."

Rachel tapped the pen she'd been using to take notes and he stared at her hand, taken again by the delicate structure of tapered fingers and pretty painted nails he would love to feel sifting through his hair, flexing against his neck, reaching for his belt…

She abruptly stopped the tapping. And then he remembered his unbecoming little speech that first day. Pat. Abrasive. Typical of the man he'd become, that didn't quite seem to be the same man within the skin that felt an inexplicable need for her touch.

"This handmaid, or guard," she said.

"Jayna."

"How do you know that she wasn't suspicious and might be setting you up?"

"Because she's under the impression I'm going to take up residence with a concubine of my own and I want to be sure said concubine has no chance of escape. Jayna's retired from the bathhouse and I'm paying her well. She has no need to be suspicious and every reason to draw a generous paycheck."

"You've been thorough."

"So have you." He smiled when she arched an expressive brow. "You checked up on me while I was gone. Were you satisfied with what you discovered?"

"I was intrigued," she admitted. "You refuse to do interviews. The business magazines say you're as much a mystery as a wunderkind. There doesn't seem to be a trace of your whereabouts until you hit the arbitrage scene eight years ago. You've been elbowing and plowing your way to the top ever since while keeping a very low profile."

"Surely you don't believe everything you read."

"No. But apparently you found out I made a few calls. I was left with the impression that you're not exactly liked by your competition, but they do respect you—like they would a piranha in a shark tank. It seems you have quite a reputation, Mr. Slick, for knowing what you want and doing whatever it takes to get it, even if that means playing dirty pool."

He usually regarded such a comment as a compliment of sorts. But coming from her, he felt a sudden need to defend himself.

"I play to win, Rachel. It's the only way I know to survive. And before you swallow someone else's sour grapes, keep in mind we're all by-products of our circumstances."

"Meaning?"

"It's not always about being better than the competition, it's about hunger, and just maybe I have reason to be hungrier than most." He could see her weighing his small confession, turning it this way and that, and emerging with something that might have been sympathy.

Sympathy for Sarah's case he wanted. Any other kind he wanted nothing of.

"Sliding that around the Rubik's Cube? Careful of the jagged edges, Rachel," he warned. "My competition is and they're way more ruthless than you."

His gaze was instinctively challenging. Guarded. But the hardness he usually felt knot in the pit of his makeup staggered against an alien force. Something that was nudging his defenses with a different kind of hunger, something inside him that said it was starved for companionship. Understanding. An open embrace that didn't come with contingencies.

Their eyes were locked. His, doubtless saying more than he could possibly bring himself to admit because the exposure, even unspoken, was tearing at years of protective masking he was urgently trying to slap back in place. Her return gaze was soft, asking for access to those hidden areas he hadn't allowed even himself to breach for so many years that it began to hurt to look at her.

Rand glanced away.

She touched his hand. He commanded himself not to grasp it and bring her into his arms.

"I hope you're not upset that I ran a check on you."

"Of course not." He chanced another meeting of eyes and met the gentlest shade of green. They could have been pastures of soft, dew kissed grass, beckoning him to rest after years of ceaseless running. "I would have been disappointed if you hadn't taken the precaution. You only proved you're careful and professional. Exactly the kind of person I need."

The person I need...I need...I need. As his words echoed with unsettling overtones, Rand felt cornered between the grinding need to yank Rachel onto his lap, and running for the front door to get the hell out while the getting was still good.

"I need to finish this file." She returned her attention to it, muttered, "I can finish sooner if you quit staring."

Glancing around her small living room as he settled deeper into her worn tapestry couch, Rand regarded the cozy warmth of flickering pillar candles in her fireplace. Beside it was a bookcase filled with more than books. How many women kept a silver flask along with a can of mace next to an old Raggedy Ann doll?

The threat of memories he was careful to keep at bay nudged at the dark corners where he kept them stored. The boy he'd once been had gotten a really bad shake. He'd lost his name along with his innocence, and as Rand stared at the doll with a missing button eye, he found himself wondering what kind of man he might have become if he hadn't left Sarah and hit the ground running.

"Thank you, sir. You saved my life."

"That depends. Just might've saved you for somethin' worse than you were running from. What's your name, boy?"

"Joshua Smith."

"Wrong. First thing you got to learn on the run is don't leave no trail. Names are like Hansel with his breadcrumbs and no bird around to eat the tracks."

Rand suppressed a shiver. It felt like a cadaver had licked the back of his neck. No wonder he never let himself think about this shit. No wonder he'd rather work 24/7 with a possessed kind of tunnel vision that kept him moving like a maniac. Work was his escape, his salvation from the somethin' worse he had raced straight into.

Still, he kept staring at Rachel's doll, wearing a faded pinafore and pantaloons, red and white stockings, little black shoes. Her hair was a mop of tangled red yarn, mouth stitched into a perpetual smile; her body was limp from much handling, declaring her well-loved and played with once upon a time.

He wondered what had happened to her eye. The one remaining seemed to wink at him, like they both knew how it felt to have a missing part.

Rand looked away. The doll gave him an odd sense of... exhaustion. Like weariness had caught up with him in the space of his pausing, and that bitch called time was blowing the whistle.

A glance at his Rolex was a welcome reminder that if he was tired, he had plenty to show for his marathon running.

It was getting late. Rachel turned the last page of the file.

He anxiously scanned her face. "So what do you think?"

"I think the findings seem accurate and the plan you outlined on hooking the slaver with me as the bait would probably work, given everything I've read."

"And given that you'll agree."

"What you're asking me to do is infiltrate a highly dangerous echelon of pleasure seekers."

"I am." He reached across the coffee table, grasped her hands. "I need you, Rachel. A number of women investigators have already turned me down. I'm working against the clock. The slavers could move their operation any day and then where would I be? Square one, scrambling to find their whereabouts that could be as close as

Reno or two thousand miles away in Atlantic City—presuming they even stick with casinos."

"And meanwhile your sister remains prisoner."

"That's right. I've already invested more time than I can afford, working out of hotels, burning up the phone wires, catching red eye flights to keep my business together. I can't do this indefinitely. Something has to happen, and fast. I've lost too much time already searching for help." He wanted to swipe away the file. He wanted this to be over. And he wanted her to know the truth. "But, Rachel, even if you turn me away, it was worth every minute just to find you."

Rachel experienced a quickening melt-down. Objectivity was essential, but she couldn't find it to save her life. And it was life as she knew it that could be on the line. Something could go wrong. She could end up in the same boat as Sarah.

She felt Rand's palms hugging hers, his grip firm and honest, flesh pressing flesh so tight it seemed the blood that flowed through his veins coursed into her own. Sarah was the only blood kin he had. If she took this case she couldn't let her mind be clouded by a major league crush on her client.

Rachel thought of how she'd spent two solid hours dolling herself up because she was all gaga over a man who wanted to hire her to save his sister. She had tried on how many outfits just so she could look like she wasn't deliberately trying to entice him, the penny loafers and ponytail a ruse to appear innocent when her entire intent was anything but. She couldn't help but feel a little ashamed of herself now that she had the full picture. While she'd had plenty of time to examine the partial file he'd overnighted several days ago, that hadn't completely prepared her for the extent of remaining information Rand had presented a few hours before.

Could she do it? Did she dare try cracking the ring when simply holding his gaze made it impossible to think?

Just the facts, ma'am, she ordered herself. She was working hard to establish her reputation, one that transcended the liability of her age. Rand was in a position to help her get a leg up.

He was also capable of compromising her ethics. *No emotional involvement allowed.* As in a heart sign with a diagonal slash. And here her heart was flipping off the slash.

As she looked at him now, all strong enigmatic male and caring desperate brother, Rachel knew if their first meeting had left her breathless, the dizzying momentum that continued to gather was enough to send her scrambling for escape from the very arms she wanted to fall into.

And that was very, *very* dangerous ground if the true purpose here was to rescue Sarah.

"You want me to work the casino, look lonely and lost. Hook up with the slaver, let him buy me a drink at the bar, lead him to think I have no family and I'm sexually innocent."

"Yes." Rand's eyes slid over her sex kitten get-up. "We might have to work on your wardrobe."

His gaze was a low simmer that said if he was going to undress her, even with his eyes, he was a very grown up man who understood the value of taking it slow.

Her body immediately responded in all the right, but oh so wrong, places. Rachel swallowed and skipped past the wardrobe part of the discussion.

"And I'd have to do the whole operation without even a gun for protection."

"The gun would raise suspicion since they'll go through your things after getting you alone. But I'll watch from a distance. And we'll bring in another PI to tail you. If you've got a colleague you prefer to work with, we'll go with your recommendation, no question."

"Jack. Jack O'Malley. He was my father's best friend and sponsored me for the five years training I had to put in before I could take the state exam. Jack is hands down great. But no matter how sharp a PI is, there's no guarantee things will go according to plan. Even Jack might not be able to get close enough to switch drinks with me." Rachel exhaled a shuddering breath. "I don't relish the thought of downing a designer drug if it comes down to that."

"And it could. I hate to spell it out, but despite any precautions, there's a good chance you will be drugged. If you are, they'll do whatever it is they do in transit and getting through that just might be easier if you're flying high or passed out. If you manage to stay sober, you'll have to give the act of your life."

"For how long?"

"The auctions take place each Saturday so it depends on when the abduction is made. Chances are you'll have at least several days of sheer hell that you've got nothing to depend on but your wits. All I can promise is that once I get you off the auction block, we'll be in this together. Even when we're staging a performance for Jayna or anyone else who might be listening at the door to what they call `The Master's Chambers.'"

Rachel gave pause to consider the implications of that. Rand, enacting his role as owner over her body. While her own body was beyond eager to get the show on the road.

Stop it, she ordered herself. Any hormonal urges or forbidden thrill she felt had no place in this moment of his dire straits and her ability to make a rational decision.

"You're sure you're in and not being set up yourself? What if it's a fake invitation and you get hauled away to a foreign prison? What if I'm stranded and go to the highest bidder? I could end up just like Sarah with no one around here to step in since you refuse to go to the FBI."

"Won't happen. My connections are paying a debt that comes to a staggering sum. My seat's reserved and I'll be watching you close. Don't worry, I've made sure the invitation's legit."

"I do worry. These go-betweens don't sound too ethical. What if they double cross you?"

"Do you actually think I'd drag you into this without having some assurance myself? We're talking heavy leverage."

"How heavy?"

"Let's just say that an unnamed third party has a sealed envelope with recognizable names, places, and lots of incriminating evidence on its way to The New York Times if there's so much as a single screw up. My 'associates' have plenty of incentive to make sure this goes off without a hitch."

A slender thread of self-preservation demanded she put up a final defense. "It's dangerous."

"I'll protect you. That's one promise I won't break."

"You said I'll be stripped. Put on an auction block." *Stripped. Auctioned off.* Could she actually endure such a violation of her modesty only to be bartered like a slab of human beef while Rand and an audience of filthy rich monsters had a clear view of her body? She shivered, imagining the ordeal.

"It's the only way. I'd never ask such a thing of anyone, and especially not you, now that I know you. But I have no choice." His grip tightened. "You can name your price. I'm willing to pay however much you ask."

For some reason that hurt. He was reducing this to money. Again. She remembered the cash he'd laid on her desk, inducing her to hear him out. Money talked. And hadn't she listened to the seductive jingle of his coin, even if she gave part of it back?

"What happens, Rand, if I say no deal?"

"Then I'll walk out and we won't see each other again—at least not under these circumstances. You might as well know that I'll try for a goodbye kiss before I hand you some hush money in exchange for your silence about everything we've discussed."

Money. Money. *Money.* As much as she needed it the thought of green bills had never been so distasteful. Just as the thought of saying goodbye to Rand was even more distressing than the idea of being publically stripped.

"But what would you do, where would you take this?"

He shrugged, a determined look spanning his face and radiating into the tenseness of his posture.

"I'd keep hunting until I found someone who would agree. I'm sure they wouldn't be half as fascinating or as impossible to look away from as you. But I have a sister to find and those are optional qualities that didn't enter the picture until now." His laugh was short, humorless. "You know, Rachel, in the too little time we've spent together, the conversations we've had when I called on any trumped up excuse just to hear your voice...Even if you don't take the case, I want to thank you for bringing some much needed light into my life."

Score. "The ink's still wet on my license, Rand."

"Doesn't matter. You're good, Rachel. Better than good. You'll be successful no matter what, but this case just might get you there a lot quicker. I have a certain amount of clout that I won't hesitate to throw in your direction if you say yes. Say it? *Say yes.*"

Rachel weighed the future ordeal against the immediate impulse chanting his plea, *Say yes.* If she did, she could reunite a sister and brother and right a terrible wrong while she took a giant leap forward in her chosen profession.

Though at the moment her profession didn't seem nearly as important as the man waiting on edge for her answer.

Once she shook on it there was no turning back.

She extended her hand.

"Put it there, partner."

CHAPTER 5

*R*and shouted a victory whoop. His hand closed over hers.

"Quite a handshake you've got, lady. Guts."

"I like yours too." She returned his beaming smile.

"Wonder what your daddy would think?"

She glimpsed another window. No daddy for Rand Slick. But he was human, wanted approval as much as the next man.

"He'd think you were no mark. He'd like you, but he wouldn't trust you. At least not with me."

"Nor should he. Sometimes I don't trust myself."

"Why not?"

Rand shrugged. "Guess it goes back to certain promises I didn't make good on. Mistakes I've made along the way."

"We all make those."

"True, but some are more irreversible than others."

She wanted to probe but his eyes told her it was private territory not to be further investigated just yet. Best to stick with a more immediate concern.

"About our roles, Rand. I think it's a good idea to get some rules in place first."

"Okay. Name them."

What rules did she want? That he wouldn't try to sleep with her when she'd lost five nights of sleep already while imagining what it would be like to get more than a little cozy with a hands-off man? She couldn't let that happen. If they crossed that line the judgement she had to keep would be toast.

"I'll think of some rules," she hedged. *Good job, Rachel! You know you can't sleep with him but that's sure not stopping you from hoping he still might go for a "let's seal the deal" kiss.*

"I have a better idea. Why don't you forget about rules for now and we give our future roles a little preliminary practice? After all, an actor doesn't just get on the stage and act his part. He studies his lines. Has his positions mapped out. I think dress rehearsals are highly advisable for our ultimate success. Don't you?"

Rachel swallowed cotton, her throat was so dry. She did not trust herself with Rand Slick. Not even with Daddy's ashes a good ten feet away in the old silver flask he'd wanted part of his remains stored in.

She averted her gaze from the flask holding court near the fireplace that burned with lit pillar candles since she couldn't afford a long overdue chimney sweep for the real thing.

"I...I guess we could give it a shot. Just don't suggest I put on a robe and give you a peek at the goods you'll be buying."

That made him laugh. As good as she was with such a tough customer maybe she should consider stand up if this PI thing didn't work out. Which could happen if she screwed things up.

"Come here." Rand patted the space on the couch beside him.

Seemed safe enough. Rachel left her chair, rounded the coffee table where the file on Sarah was spread out. But just as she was about to sit where indicated, Rand pulled her onto his lap.

Her behind landed squarely on something of substance that had her gasp of surprise colliding with a low, masculine groan.

"Mmm. Much better. You give good concubine."

"Rand!"

"Call me Master." His fingers threaded through her ponytail, pulled back with a most masterful tug. While his command had been playful, there was something deeply serious going on between their meeting of eyes. "Go ahead," he urged. "Say it."

She hesitated. Then whispered, "Master."

"Oh, I like that."

And apparently he did, judging from what was being transmitted from his lap to hers.

Her attempt to get up was more like a squirm of indecision.

Rand clamped a strong palm over a thigh that had begun to shake and whispered, "Be still."

Was he kidding? How was she supposed to be still when his lips were suddenly skating her exposed neck while the hand in her hair loosened the scarf she had artfully arranged to play hide-and-seek with her upswept curls?

"I'm not sure if this is such a good idea, Rand," she managed to get out. "Maybe we should just ad lib when the time comes."

His answer was a deeper nuzzle to her neck, then a looping wrap of her freed scarf around her wrists. He didn't try to tie it but she didn't feel any less bound by the desire the action provoked, augmented by the wild leap of her pulse when he quietly urged, "Hook your arms around my neck and tell me what you really want."

What did she *really* want? She wanted to do exactly as he'd asked. She wanted to inhale the marvelous scent of him forever. She wanted to rip off his clothes and see everything her hands, her entire body, wanted to feel all over her. She wanted to wake up next to him and watch him shave after his five o'clock shadow had rubbed her raw in all the places that begged to have him there now. *Now.*

But *now* was only just that. *Now* was not tomorrow or the next day or the day after that. *Now* didn't care about the consequences of immediate gratification, let the future take care of itself.

Welcome to Vegas, baby. Vegas was a good teacher. So was her daddy. And if he had taught her anything it was that there was no free lunch. You danced to the music, you paid the piper one way or another. And of course there was always the admonition to "keep your britches up and don't let me down."

She wasn't worried about letting Daddy down. He was in a flask in her bookcase. Her real concern was letting herself down, and she was really close to it, because more than anything she wanted to forget that Rand Slick was her first big client and if this went any further, that was a real slippery slope she didn't have the professional, or personal, experience to navigate.

"What do you want?" he murmured again. "Tell me."

"I want you to look at me."

He did and those windows that guarded his eyes were like black magic beckoning her in.

"You want me to help you get your sister back, don't you?"

He nodded. Windows a little less hazy.

"Rand, there's something you have to understand. A private investigator can't get emotionally involved with a client. It's just asking for big trouble. I'm already more emotionally involved than I should be, and I think maybe so are you. It's like a patient who's attached to a doctor but the doctor has to keep some distance because he could risk a patient's safety if he's got his head in the clouds—or is thinking with his britches."

"Britches?" Rand repeated. His lips twitched.

She nodded.

"Mine have been too tight for comfort ever since you opened the door. What about yours?"

"My britches are not your concern." She didn't sound convincing even to herself. She *had* to get off his lap, and mean it.

"Not so fast."

He pulled her back down and in one smooth move had her scarf-looped wrists around his neck while his hand on her skintight cigarette pants inched up until the tip of a masculine finger lightly flirted with some embarrassingly wet polyester. "Judging from the state of your britches, Ms. Tinsdale, I'd say that they're very much my concern."

She'd been kissed. She'd been fondled. But she'd never encountered anything like this. She was way off her turf while Rand was obviously in his element.

Oh yeah, he was definitely the bad boy that Daddy had warned her about. Bad boys liked good girls. Only good girls weren't so good anymore once they gave up their goods. And PI's who forgot they really were like a doctor in a patient's time of need stood a very good chance of not only bombing a case but being devastated themselves if the case was solved and their client's attachment was no longer so personal.

Rachel got her arms off his neck, shook loose the scarf from her wrists, and gripped the knowing hand that was proving way too capable of threatening her resolve.

"I'm not easy, Rand."

"I never thought that you were."

"Then prove it by removing your hand from my privates and letting me sign the agreement papers. We'll pretend that this didn't happen, shake on our deal, and say a polite goodnight."

CHAPTER 6

*R*and eschewed valet service and pulled his latest rental into a designated VIP slot. He killed the engine but let the CD continue to play.

God, he had some thinking to do. The way Rachel smelled, the way she felt on his hands, against his mouth. When he'd finally touched her it was almost surreal, like he was in the midst of a wet dream with his dream girl.

And he still hadn't kissed her. At least not on the mouth. After their abrupt departure from the couch they had signed the agreement papers—with an adjustment from Rachel to the terms. He had already penciled in $250,000 for payment and invited her to negotiate up. Rachel crossed out a 0 and revised his offer to read: "$25,000 retainer plus expenses and fair compensation TBD upon delivery of services rendered."

They shook on the deal. But if she thought there was any way that either of them would forget what had happened on her couch, she was terribly mistaken. As they shook hands a little longer than necessary, he had leaned down and the look in her eyes, saying so clearly *I know what I said but kiss me anyway,* did something unexpected to his intentions. Everything about her was so fresh and new, he'd almost felt like a schoolboy stealing his first kiss.

On her cheek.

It was an enormous novelty. So innocent but knowing. So packed with the possibilities of experiencing some of what he'd missed in his youth.

"I would apologize for what happened if I was sorry," he'd told her. "But I'm not. Are you?"

Her silence was answer enough.

And the last thing he said was, "Goodnight, Angel."

He had called her Angel. It just slipped out. Endearments weren't his style, and Angel was the most treasured of all. That's when he knew. He was hooked. And he wanted more of what she'd said they couldn't have.

Was he concerned that an emotional entanglement could jeopardize their mission? A little. Maybe. But he wasn't convinced. Besides, they were already emotionally entangled. Not to mention generating enough sexual heat to nearly combust on contact. And that was *not* going away.

Rand sniffed his fingertips, then stroked his bottom lip. *The better to taste you with, my dear.* The wolf in him definitely had the hots for Little Miss Red. But Little Miss Red had said "no" and he had honored that.

He could be exceptionally disciplined when he had to be, or chose to be. There was even a possibly sick part of him that found self-deprivation gratifying, almost enjoyable, maybe because it had defined so much of his life. And so...

For the time being, he could, and would, behave. Or at least appear to while ramping up the attraction between them that was already off the charts insane. Just a whiff of her scent made the control freak he was feel a little crazy, so it wouldn't be easy.

"I'm not easy, Rand."

"I never thought that you were."

He put the finger that had touched "her privates" to his tongue. He did not particularly envy Rachel being the object of his absolute desire. He was a guy with a load of damaged baggage. If he stumbled, he could come down on her like a house of old bricks that weren't well shored up by the foundation they were built on.

No one knew better than he just how battered that foundation was. It's why he was always doing a Paul Simon with "50 Ways To Leave Your Lover" before he conked out after a tryst. But for all the lovers he'd had, he didn't have a lot of experience with actual intimacy. He knew that about himself. Just like he knew the reason he had never really *slept* with anyone was because he didn't want to risk them hearing him scream.

A couple strolled by, unaware he was watching. They were middle aged and had the kind of body language that suggested long familiarity, not a just hooked up one night stand. The man was patting her behind; she was laughing. And then she turned, gave him her mouth, and after a short kiss he went for a breast, only for her to swat his hand away. They laughed together and then went on to find their car and no doubt a little more pleasure under the covers of a bed that wasn't rented for a night.

He wanted some of that. Badly. And what was so amazing was that it was the first time in his life that he was envious of strangers who just might wake up in the morning and wonder how they could pay their kid's college tuition and still have enough to retire in ten years.

Rand shut off the CD, got out of the car. He always put off calling it a day as long as possible. The night had not been his friend for a very long time—that's when the little demons liked to come out and play. Usually. Rachel's voice had interrupted some of his nightmares this week.

Once in his room, he stared at the bed that she would not be sharing.

"It's like a patient who's attached to a doctor but the doctor has to keep

some distance because he could risk a patient's safety if he's got his head in the clouds—or is thinking with his britches."

Britches. She had him at *britches*. No, she'd had him before then, the britches just licked the envelope and sealed it.

Rand stripped off his clothes and wondered how he could feel 60 and 16 all at once. As his eyes drifted shut and he imagined getting her into the backseat of a Buick while make out music spilled from the dashboard, he knew this wasn't just about saving Sarah anymore. She had to come first, he couldn't forget that. But arbitrage, the thing he excelled at, was about making a profit by juggling commodities and making split second decisions without dropping the ball or losing your nerve. It was all about risk and reward.

If he did this right, not only would he get Sarah back, Rachel just might help him find a long lost boy by the name of Joshua Smith.

CHAPTER 7

*R*achel put the finishing touches on her makeup and debated between a tiny perfume bottle and the little crystal atomizer holding her favorite fragrance. *Tweed*. What she had was from the 50's or maybe the 60's—the original version. Sometime after that the formula had changed and it didn't smell quite the same, so she was careful with how much she used of her limited supply.

A little spritz behind each ear. Another little spritz into her cleavage. She hesitated then quickly spritzed a shot up her little black dress. It felt like a secret sin.

Shave and a haircut, two bits. Rachel glanced at the charm bracelet that Rand had given her—a dainty handmade piece of jewelry with little charms that had completely charmed her amidst a dangling timepiece she quickly checked.

Eight o'clock on the nose. She could set her clock by the man, he was so punctual.

Rand had proven to be a lot of things in the month that they had been perfecting their sting operation with Jack. It had been an exhilarating, exhausting month of planning strategy, scouting casinos, enacting dry runs to get their timing just right...and spending a lot of energy pretending there wasn't something so electric between her and Rand that all they had to do was lock eyeballs for green and brown to turn hazel while the oxygen was sucked from the room.

Even now she felt a little dizzy as she opened the front door and there he stood in a dark tailored suit, perfectly cinched tie, crisp white shirt, monogramed **RS** on the cuffs, and fine leather shoes—with cashmere socks, no doubt. He'd been some kind of eye candy the moment they met, but somehow he just kept turning into even more of a dreamboat each time she saw him. Maybe because he kept letting her see a little bit more and then a little bit more of what was under the surface. Such a tease.

Rand's eyes glinted appreciatively as he looked her over from her French twist up-do, to the simple black cocktail dress that prudently came to just above her knees, to the open-toed pumps with a tiny tracking device embedded beneath the sole.

From behind his back he produced a single red rose.

"Roses are red. Violets are blue. It's the Big Bad Wolf and he's got a thing for you." He tickled her nose with the petals.

Rachel laughed nervously. "Let me get my purse and—"

"And we need to talk before you do that. May I come in, or do I need to do some huffing and puffing first?"

"You can huff and puff all that you like, but we don't have time to talk. Tonight's show time and Jack's already waiting. He called me from the casino and said he was calling you next. Did he?"

"He did. That's why we need to talk."

Rand moved past her, elbowed the door shut, and leaned against it, barring their exit.

She was terribly afraid that she knew what this was about.

"Rand? We need to go."

She turned, intent on grabbing the little black bag filled with a small amount of cash, a tube of lipstick, fake ID, and another tiny tracking device sewn into the lining.

He caught her arm. She stared at the connection of olive skin against her own pale flesh. Where his fingertips touched turned to liquid fire spreading through her veins and pumping through her blood until she thought the dynamite burning at both ends would explode.

"It's not too late, Angel," Rand said quietly. "You can still back out. Do it."

Knowing how much his sister meant to him, she could only meet his probing stare with a determined shake of her head, the careful touch of her fingertips to his brutally handsome face.

"Do you actually think, even for a minute, that I would?"

"No, but I want you to reconsider before it's too late. If Jack's right and he's spotted our quarry, you could be on your way to only God knows what in a matter of hours. Now that the time could be here, I can't stand the thought of subjecting you to that."

"Then don't think it. Just think about us hitting pay dirt and a week from now we could be in Zebedique, doing what we're there to do—saving Sarah. It's what you hired me for. I'm prepared."

"I'm not. When I first came into your office you were a means to an end. Things have changed."

In one svelte move he had their places exchanged. Her against the door, shoulders pressed against it by his palms, rose discarded to the floor.

"Tell me you're off the case." His mouth hovered whisper close. "I don't want you to go through with this. I'll find someone else and—"

"Stop it, Rand. Stop it!" Rachel pushed at his chest. It wasn't moving, only bearing so close her fists were caught between their upper torsos while he cupped her behind and hoisted her up so that their hips were locked and her sweet spot was all but French kissing his fly.

"Wrap your legs around me. You know you want to."

"It doesn't matter what I want. I told you we couldn't get emotionally involved. If this doesn't prove my point, nothing does. You have a sister who needs you, who needs me because I can get to her where you can't. And not only her, what about the other women at risk while you shop for someone to take my place?"

"I don't know those other women. I don't care about them. You, I care about."

"Don't. Care later, Rand. Care when you can afford to." She managed to work her hands free, gripped his shoulders, and tried to shake some sense into them both. "Once you have Sarah back and this case is closed, you'll be thanking me with a paycheck for services rendered and no obligation beyond that."

Dark windowed eyes narrowed. His lips closed in.

"Kiss me. If you can kiss me and still say that, I won't fight you on a decision that you should not make."

She'd already made her decision. It didn't stop her from planting her mouth against his like she'd imagined a thousand times before, only to realize he tasted even better than she ever imagined and Rand Slick didn't kiss back like anything she'd been prepared for.

His mouth was dark magic that pulled up moans from her throat and seduced every thought, every nerve end to a point of such deliriously sweet torture, she felt drugged already. And then his mouth was no longer on hers, it was everywhere else. In her hair, on her neck, then whispering into her ear those words again, "Wrap your legs around me" while he cinched up the hem of her little black dress until it was riding her waist and she felt nothing between them but her panties and stockings and the seam of his zipper.

She couldn't stop herself. She wrapped her legs around him and her secret sin of an atomizing spritz wafted into the scent of lust drunk air rising from his slow rhythmic thrusts against her drenched panties. She could feel her body opening into a hungry yawn and moving with his—until her hips took on a life of their own, uncontrollably thrusting back.

And then the indescribable happened that had her writhing against the wall, tearing at his hair, tearing her mouth away from his because she couldn't breathe beyond the release of a keening *"Rand!"* before she collapsed in the arms that held her against him.

"There," he said hoarsely. "There. We have it settled now. I'll call Jack. Tell him we're scrapping the plan. Then we'll pick this up on our new terms. I'm no longer your client. And you're no longer the bait for anyone but me."

Rachel sucked in unsteady breaths. She unclamped her thighs from his waist and tried to stand on her own steam only for her trembling legs to give way.

"I've got you." He pressed his lips against her no longer carefully coifed hair and breathed again, "I've got you."

His assurance was gentle, but beneath it she detected the authoritative sound of a man who was accustomed to calling the shots.

Somehow amidst all the internal organs that were still quivering, Rachel found her balance. She pushed down the little black dress that she never should have let him pull up, and prayed she could get her vocal chords to work beyond a continuing sequence of gasps.

When she spoke her voice was surprisingly steady, and the spine that was no longer getting softly banged against the door, pure steel.

"Save yourself the call, Mr. Slick. We're running late. We have a slaver to catch. Find your car keys while I tidy myself up and get my purse."

Rand scanned the crowd in the casino until his gaze connected with Jack's. Jack gave a small nod before moving to a gaming table a discreet distance from where Rachel stood.

It was taking all that he had not to grab her and *run, Rand, run.* There were few things he hated more than feeling control slip from his grip, which had become rare. It was an actual, awful physical sensation: His fingers cold and feeling like they were clawing at an iron door, his body banging against a train car while the velocity of wind tried to suck him down and under slicing death wheels.

Outwardly he had trained himself to look as impassive as he appeared now when Rachel bent closer to a roulette wheel. But inwardly was a whole other story. His heart hammered against his ribs and a sick feeling churned in the pit of his stomach. When Rachel slid him a sidelong glance, then turned the smile that belonged to him on a man who sidled up beside her...

Rand's grip tightened so hard around his rocks glass it was a wonder he didn't feel the bite of shards cutting into the hand that should still be on her—

After he dealt with the dick who was wearing enough gold chains to put Fort Knox out of business and had a motor mouth that wouldn't quit. No way was this asshole their target.

Asshole rested a palm on a smooth ivory shoulder. Rand crunched ice and didn't care if he broke a molar.

To his relief, Rachel cut the touchy-feely short and headed for a Black Jack table. Jack cut his losses and moved in closer. Rand cut through the crowd, tailing her at a judicious distance.

His attention eventually focused on an elegant man who could pass for Prince Charles in evening attire approaching Rachel with a questioning smile. He appeared to be confused as he asked her something. When Rachel responded, the man shrugged expressively and shook his head, his smile so charming and sincere it made Rand immediately suspicious.

As Prince Charming continued to engage Rachel in what seemed an entertaining conversation, Rand placed his glass on a passing cocktail tray and bent down, pretending to tie his shoe. From his peripheral vision he could see pretty pink toenails peeking out from black pumps with an embedded tracking device yet another PI was monitoring from a high roller suite in the casino.

Rand's gaze slid up shapely legs that should still be around his waist. *Goddammit.* Why hadn't she listened to him? What if he had been double crossed somehow, or she was raped en route, or the plane went down, or she just disappeared and never showed up at the hateful auction he never should have begged her to agree to?

"Stop it, Rand. Stop it! I told you we couldn't get emotionally involved. If this doesn't prove my point, nothing does. You have a sister who needs you, who needs me because I can get to her where you can't."

Rand took a deep breath, stood. Where was the lean, mean money machine who could cut off his emotions in a blink? He'd begun to think that Rachel was making him a better man, but at the moment, he didn't consider it such an improvement.

As he discreetly took note of the too smooth moves from an oily operator, and Jack's seasoned eye for a con sent a curt nod to concur, Rand felt a prickle at the back of his neck. The prickle spread while Rachel played her role with a flawless finesse, appearing interested but not overly eager.

Prince baby gestured toward the bar and Rachel was just-right hesitant before slowly smiling in agreement.

When she dropped her sequined purse, the sign they just might have hit the jackpot, the prickle turned into a small army of termites swarming under his skin.

In the space of a few seconds that stretched into eternity as their target stooped down to retrieve her purse, Rachel shot him a sharp glare with the unmistakable warning: *Don't you dare screw this up.*

He'd once thought she was kittenish, but never again. What he saw was a she-cat swinging her attention to their mark, and sinking her claws into him like a pro.

If Rachel was afraid she wasn't showing it while his own heart banged hard enough to drown out the cacophony of slots hitting *ka-ching, ka-ching, ka-ching.*

Rand casually followed them into the bar and immediately scoped out some obvious company-for-hire sitting all alone in a red leather corner booth. She readily invited him to join her, buy her a drink, while he watched Jack beat someone to the barstool beside the one Rachel had taken, so she was sandwiched between him and the slaver.

It had to be the slaver.

As Rand watched her doing her job, so incredibly well she deserved an Oscar, he did a double take.

For an instant he could have sworn Rachel wasn't dressed to kill in black, but was naked beneath a swath of gossamer white.

CHAPTER 8

*R*achel's stomach rolled over for the hundredth time in ten minutes. The cucumber cool she'd felt in rehearsal was nowhere to be found as she confronted the real thing. *Help, Rand! You were right, this is too scary and I want out!* She battled the instinct to high-tail it into his arms that were less than twenty feet away despite the clear message she had sent with a glare to keep his distance—which she should have demanded earlier since the intoxicating madness of his kiss, his body making hers come undone, were like opioids that were still in her system.

Since she hadn't been able to separate what had happened then from what had to happen now, she decided to use it to her benefit. The glow in her face was real. So was the secret smile on her lips, the barely banked fire that still glistened in her eyes.

Maurice, as he had introduced himself, was entranced. Or at least he appeared to be, unless he was doing some acting himself, as she tilted her head so the soft lighting would play her hair to its best red advantage.

"Beautiful hair on a beautiful lady," Maurice said, his voice dripping enough culture for Barrymore and Olivier combined. He was so convincing that she might have bought it if her trained eye hadn't spotted some subtleties that marked him as a counterfeit:

His nails were clean but needed clipping, along with a few nose hairs. His shoes could use a shine. A missing button on his shirt. Tarnished belt buckle. Cologne, too strong. Little things, telling things. A man of true wealth and breeding would have seen to the finishing touches. Like Rand.

Rachel flicked her eyes down, pretending a demure acceptance of Maurice's admiration. He could use some new socks, too. Cashmere they were not.

"I'm glad you like my hair. But really, Maurice, such an outrageous compliment, no wonder I'm blushing."

"Don't tell me you don't get at least a dozen a day. As for your blush, such a rarity. You have remarkable skin. Actually, I think it the most beautiful skin I've ever seen."

She looked shyly away, her gaze brushing Rand's from across the room where he made small talk with a hooker. The momentary connection steeled her resolve and escalated her running pulse to a gallop. Her cheeks went from a glow to a hot burn as she noticed Maurice's quick, calculating assessment of her bosom. Rachel pressed an unsteady hand to her cleavage, hoping the material would absorb the trickling beads of sweat.

"Oh, Maurice, you're too kind. You can't be serious!"

"But my dear," he said, laughing softly, "I have never been more serious. You are, in fact, *exquisite*. I'm a worldly man, in experience not to mention travel. But my acquaintance with women of your ilk—intelligent, beautiful beyond words, and such an entertaining conversationalist—is, shall we say, unfortunately limited. Surely you've had many men, besides myself, appreciate those attributes."

"Oh, no. No! Actually, well...my parents would be appalled if they knew I was here, getting acquainted with a gentleman as worldly as yourself."

"Parents?" he asked, leaning slightly away.

Rachel shook her head. Sadly. "I miss them so much. It was a car accident two years ago. They were so wonderful, even if overly protective."

"But what about brothers, sisters? Grandparents, aunts or uncles? Surely you're not all alone."

"If I wasn't, I wouldn't be here. Celebrating my birthday, all by my lonesome, and hoping a new job comes through before I run out of my inheritance. I'm afraid it wasn't much."

"Then you have no job, no family, or friends who should be here with you?"

She shrugged, making her shoulders an unspoken invitation along with the breasts she pressed closer together to increase the volume they didn't really need.

"Maurice, I hate to admit it, but for some reason I feel safe telling you. My life is just kind of a lonely mess right now, and you have no idea how much I appreciate meeting such a genuinely nice—and very handsome—gentleman who makes me feel not nearly as alone as I did before you intro-duced yourself. I came to the casino because I didn't want to sing 'It's my birthday and I can cry if I want to' in a hotel room." She paused, shook her head. "Oh, you might as well know it all. I was evicted from my apartment last week and—"

"My dear, how tragic! I'm so glad you told me. You deserve so much better. Here now, let me order a bottle of champagne and we'll toast to you. To us!" The glint in his eyes reminded her of matching fruit rolling up on a slot machine and spitting out a stream of silver that he greedily fingered as he raised a single finger to the bartender that had thus far stayed too busy to acknowledge them.

Rachel scrambled for a believable response. "Champagne sounds wonderful, but Maurice, it goes straight to my head. Maybe just a glass of Chardonnay?" Now that Jack had been delivered his, despite arriving shortly after her and Maurice, maybe they could still make the exchange.

"Whatever your heart desires, my new friend. Whatever your heart desires."

Maurice placed the order, a Chardonnay for her and a Scotch rocks for him, without specifying Macallan or another fine vintage as Rand would, further separating a truly upscale partaker from a fraud.

Not that she needed further confirmation at this point.

Rachel realized she had begun to shake her foot and disguised the action by tugging down the hem that had ridden above her knees an uncomfortable few inches. Maurice's appreciative notation of the small act suggested that he more than liked her sense of modesty. He was lapping it up. The creep. Chances were he was sizing up the status of her virginity and the bonus money it would bring if her damn hymen was intact.

Refusing to consider the inevitable investigation of her body, Rachel managed to quell the queasy swish of her stomach and leaned back so that Jack was a few inches closer for the little while longer she had him to count on.

Maurice kept the conversation running with an anecdote she laughed at in all the right places while stolen glances alerted her that the bartender fixed her companion's libation in clear sight, but took a half-minute too long to pour her simple glass of Chardonnay beneath the counter's ledge.

Drugged. The wine glass he sat before her with a flourish and a smile was drugged. Rachel deflected her immediate impulse to recoil from Maurice and dump the drink in his lap. She could feel Rand's gaze on her back and with it came the familiar tickle of fine hairs dancing on her nape. He was anxious, worried, and sending her a silent message that it wasn't too late to get out.

Rachel reached for her glass, meaning to slide it a few crucial inches closer to Jack's identical goblet.

Maurice caught her trembling fingertips with his own that were smooth, dry, and insistent. He inhaled the liquid bouquet before moving it beneath her nose.

"Roses are red. Violets are blue. It's the big bad wolf and he's got a thing for you."

Rose tickling her nose. Rose to the floor…

Rachel accepted the glass. She remembered the way Rand had laughed at her dad's silly toast, and now she beamed at the memory, at all the others, that would get her through this acid test, the genuine terror of what was almost certainly coming next.

"A sip and a toast. To you, my sweet, and especially to our most fortuitous meeting."

A quick glance to the left and she saw their bartender disappear through a swish of nearby ruby velvet doors. Her educated guess was that he had a fast call to make and a driver would be meeting them at the entrance.

Rachel pretended to take a small drink then sat the glass next to Jack, just as they'd planned. What they hadn't planned on was Maurice's quick retrieval and his admonishing shake of the head while he urged the rim to her lips.

"Come now, you don't *really* consider that to do justice to your birthday or our delightful acquaintance, do you? Let's try this again. To you. To me. To a night we'll never forget."

Had Jack switched the glasses? Not unless he was faster than David Copperfield and Houdini rolled into one.

"Here, here!" Rachel faked another sip. Before she could land the glass on the bar and stall for a few precious seconds, Maurice caught her wrist and tilted, tilted….

Deciding if she didn't drink up she'd risk blowing their cover, Rachel took several quick swallows. It had a slight bitter flavor, but otherwise there was no telltale taste.

Maybe she was better off drugged than enduring more of this hell that she knew was nothing compared to the hell awaiting her.

At least this way she wouldn't have to fake the effects. *Let it hit*, she decided.

The effects kicked in before she could polish off half the glass. Something tickled the back of her throat and emerged as a silly giggle. Maurice was stroking her calf with his unshiny shoe tip that had begun to gleam like Tinkerbell's wand in the shimmering darkness. And how agreeable she felt when he whispered they should blow this joint and hit the town in style.

Sounded good to her. But it shouldn't. Rachel frowned, then laughed as she scrambled for a wisp of comprehension. The room grew languorously hazy and so did her brain. She reached for her purse and knocked it to the floor.

"I'll get it, my dear," Maurice graciously offered, swiping it up and leading her out on his arm.

If she was going to be drugged, Rachel decided this one wasn't half bad. She laughed gaily, feeling wildly uninhibited and loose. Everything struck her as funny:

The way Jack was getting up and taking her glass along with him. And Maurice patting her purse that he wouldn't find a gun in. Of course in her current state of hilarious insanity she'd think it real funny to blow his friggin' head off if she had her favorite Glock. Best birthday present ever.

She would have liked to say as much but her tongue felt plumper than an overstuffed quilt.

As they made their exit from the bar she was aware of an electric sensation stitching up her spine. Someone had touched the small of her back.

Even flying high she didn't need to look to see who it was. Only one person had ever affected her like that. Rachel tilted her spinning head and caught a parting glance from Rand before he was swallowed by the crowd zooming in, out, then whirling round and round in telescopic Technicolor.

Unlike her, Rand hadn't been smiling. So what, she thought as another lilting giggle erupted. Those stern lips of his were made for kissing like crazy and, crazy as she was for him, she'd gladly return his dumb dough in exchange for another taste of that gorgeous, sexy mouth.

She hoped he hurried up and met her in...well, wherever the heck he was going to buy her. Too bad it was going to cost him when she was already his for free.

Rand could not remember the last time he'd been in such a twisting-in-the-wind kind of agony. His well-honed ability to divorce himself from emotion was nowhere to be found as he went dumpster diving—only this time for something other than somebody's scraps to call his own dinner.

He and Jack had trailed the slaver and Rachel from the casino, with him driving and Jack on the phone with his associate in the suite, tracking her as long as possible before traffic cut them off from a few cars behind. It wasn't like they were going to nab Rachel back and hold the slaver at gun point at whatever destination the slaver's car stopped, but simply losing sight of them had dealt what felt like a double fisted blow to Rand's gut.

Now here they were near a private airstrip, not even a plane's blinking lights taking to the air to assure him that Rachel had been hoisted safely away. All he had was the best technology money could buy indicating Rachel's last traces were tossed away in this dumpster...somewhere.

"Any luck?" Jack shouted.

Rand had to wonder what luck meant when you were picking through garbage and praying you wouldn't find a body—then shuddering in relief to find a pair of women's shoes.

Rand held them momentarily, keeping them all to himself as he rubbed the insoles where her feet had been.

Reluctantly, he gave them up.

"Catch!" he called, flinging them over the side before digging and clawing around the general area until he latched onto what felt like a purse.

Holding it in his cold hands, the light of the moon confirmed it was the sequined vintage clutch he had bought in New York, the same day he'd gone to Tiffany's and had a little charm bracelet made with tiny platinum trinkets to convey things he couldn't express but had hoped Rachel would take as a sign of his affections that went far beyond their professional alliance.

As he stood there in the dumpster, Rand unclasped the burnished gold latch and took careful stock: The little bit of cash and the fake ID were gone. The same lipstick he'd eaten off her lips was there in a gold push-up tube, and...*what was this?*

A tiny bottle of perfume.

Tweed was etched across the glass. Beneath it read:

Lentheric

*London * Paris * New York*

Rand fingered the bottle he couldn't remember seeing before yet looked somehow familiar, and carefully twisted off the gold cap, feeling as if a genie might emerge.

What emerged was the scent that was Rachel. The smell of her that drove him absolutely wild—but now made him feel crazed in a completely different way. This was all he had left of her while she was drugged and in the hands of some seriously bad people because of the trajectory of circumstances he had set in motion over twenty years before.

If hindsight was 20/20 there were so many things he would undo. Too late for that now. All he had was bone deep regret and gut churning fear that his best laid plans to save Sarah could be at Rachel's expense.

Don't think it. You'll go crazy if you do, and you have to keep your shit together.

Rand pocketed the little bottle of *Tweed.* He tossed Rachel's purse over to Jack's waiting hands, and hoisted himself out of the dumpster.

Jack pulled a handkerchief from his slightly rumpled suit coat to mop a forehead that looked like it had logged every mile on a map from Nevada to New York.

"Jeezus, I'm telling ya, if anything happens to that girl, her daddy's gonna make sure hell looks like heaven once we meet up again."

"I'm in hell already." Rand suddenly wondered if his charm bracelet had been discarded with the rest. The only thing that stopped him from climbing back into the dumpster was knowing the bracelet could be replaced and time was too valuable to waste.

"Your private plane's waiting." Jack did a little more brow mopping. "Lemme know when you land."

"Will do. Anything else?"

"Yeah." Jack pushed his sweaty handkerchief under Rand's nose and advised him, "Smell this. If you don't bring our girl home safe and sound, all the hounds in hell got nothin' on what's coming down on you. You dig?"

"I dig." Rand didn't need Jack to say more. If Rachel wasn't on that auction block in Zebedique next Saturday, it was all on him. And he truly did not know how any man could live with the knowledge of losing not only his sister, but a woman who was making him wonder if even a bad penny like him could learn how to love.

CHAPTER 9

A finely embroidered linen tunic with a mandarin collar matched the loose trousers that slightly flapped against Rand's sandal-clad feet. He quickened his paces, sidestepping a peddler hawking gaudy jewelry from a brightly colored cart. A drunk, thrown from a tavern's swinging doors, landed in his path.

Stepping over him without a cursory glance, Rand's mind remained locked on Rachel. The ears he had to the ground and eyes wherever he could buy them indicated that a stunning young red head was in the pool of newly imported love slaves that were going up for auction.

A queasy feeling twisted his insides with each thought of what the slavers might have done to her. His utter impotence to help her when she'd needed him the most was a bitter reminder of past failure.

Shutting out what he didn't need reminding of, Rand concentrated on his surroundings: Zebedique. Just as he remembered it. Beggars and whores and stinking rich sultans milled through the narrow cobblestone streets that were lined with casinos and massage parlors, opium dens and exquisite jewelry stores.

It was a twenty-four-hour party as rich as it was sleazy. The smell of spice and incense permeated everything. He caught himself sniffing his pores as he rounded a familiar corner and headed straight for a voluptuous building composed of stained glass windows and swirling gold turrets that looked like butter-scotch dipped Dairy Queen Cones.

Rand adjusted his purple and gold skullcap with tiny diamond-like mirrors sewn in to resemble a crown. Lots of royalty around here—especially if you counted various kingpins of industry.

"You are invited?" the guard said in broken English.

Luckily, English was used as the link of communication amongst the global gathering represented in Zebedique. Rand had no reason to hire an interpreter, as many here did, or to pretend he was anything but what he was: A visiting American with enough money and contacts to grant him entry to this high roller den of iniquity. Even so, he'd studied up on the local dialect and could get by.

"I am invited. Do you wish to see my papers?" Upon a nod from the guard, Rand produced a letter of introduction and proof of an unlimited line of credit at a Swiss bank.

The guard waved him inside. As he took his indicated seat, Rand declined a drink and the sexual favors a servant girl offered. He scanned the crowd, aware that anticipation seemed to pulse through the air of what reminded him of an opulent theater that housed perhaps two hundred attendees in a semi-circle around a gleaming wood stage. Fat men, handsome men, old goats and fast livers lounged and drank and greedily fondled the girls that were in ample supply; low murmurs filtered through the musical strains of a flute.

A loud clap sounded from the stage. The flute was joined by a sitar. And out came a line of exotic heavily made-up women in sequined brassieres and bottoms pieced together like maypole ribbons. Tempting glimpses of flesh were revealed as they began to dance and undulate in a sinuous choreography until they had formed the semblance of an inner and outer set of lips—the unmistakable likeness of a vulva.

So this was how the slavers worked up their customers, Rand thought almost dazedly. This wasn't Vegas strutting its brassy stuff. And it wasn't porn, graphically manipulating the base line of primal instinct. No. This was in a class of sexual stimulation all by itself and Rand wished he could say he was immune.

As he watched the dancers slowly strip off their provocative costumes to reveal bronzed bodies glistening with oil, he could only envision Rachel, her fair skin, flowing red hair, and lips lush with invitation beckoning him to take her home. And when the dancers began to fondle themselves while the music rhythmically pulsed with their movements, he imagined Rachel's legs were still wrapped around him and he had her against the wall, pretending there wasn't anything between the solid bump and grind of their hips until she—

Rand groaned, feeling the rush of his blood, the almost poignant rise of his responding erection. His groan was echoed by many and he wished to heaven they'd just get on with it.

He got his wish. The women finished their dance and left. A dark, sinewy gnome of a man, who reminded him of an exotically clad monkey amidst a lewd coterie of organ grinders, took center stage.

The room, charged with lust, went silent.

"Bring the girl out." He clapped his hands twice and two simi-larly costumed men struggled with a dark, slender woman who was twisting and screaming and trying to break free of their hold in spite of the bright pink silken binding wrapped around her wrists.

Rand had seen the bad side of life; he'd seen worse than ugly. This appalled even him. The rest of the crowd was thrilled, judging from the murmur of approval sweeping through the room.

"She is spirited," noted the auctioneer. "A fine Egyptian woman to warm a man's bed." He signaled and a large ruby encrusted gold hook attached to a pulley dropped from the top of the stage. With obvious practice the two assistants looped the binding between her wrists over the hook and left. With another signal the rope raised from the pulley until she was balanced on her toes.

The woman was openly crying, begging for mercy, and Rand toyed with the notion of buying her just so he could set her free.

He couldn't. There were going to be a lot more women exactly like her and buying each one was out of the question.

"You like her breasts?" said the gnome. "Then see how you like the rest!" With a jerk of his hand he whipped the sheet from her body, exposing her in full frontal nudity.

The woman shrieked while the audience applauded.

"Unfortunately she is not a virgin." The gnome caught her around the waist, the rope turning with his pivot. "But she is very tight and why should virginity matter with such beautiful buttocks, and thighs you can train to wrap around your own?"

The bidding lasted several minutes while the auctioneer upped each one, constantly extolling her merits.

She sold for the equivalent of fifty thousand dollars. The owner claimed her. Amidst polite applause he carried her off the stage.

Rand wished he'd taken the drink he'd been offered. He needed something to get a hold on himself before Rachel was similarly disgraced. Something to dampen this sick anticipation. He couldn't bear the thought of seeing her so horribly handled, of these other men looking upon her while they fondled themselves and placed their bids.

While he would outbid each one and doubtless be filling himself up with the sight of her nakedness.

The thought left him with a load of self-disgust. And the familiar arousal that thoughts of her always evoked. By the fifth girl the two warring qualities had twisted together with his gnawing anxiety: overt references to sex, nudity, and concern over Rachel bombarded his senses.

"And now gentlemen, the most intoxicating beauty we have ever offered. American. Educated. And best of all—" He clapped his hands and Rand watched, numb and yet, as he had feared he would be, hideously enthralled as Rachel was led onto the stage, her own silk bindings pure white. "She is a *virgin!*"

Flanked by the guards, she held her head high and silently walked with nothing but a sheet and her attitude to the center of the platform. Rand could see her scanning the crowd, eyes guarded but alert.

Good God she was glorious, standing proud and aloof from it all. He sensed the other patrons' anticipation, the excitement sweeping them into a taut, hushed frenzy of lust.

Rand lusted too. Her eyes caught his and he knew she was pleading with him to end this quickly and take her away from this horrible place. Unable to stop himself, his gaze dipped to the sheet that covered the body he would ensure no one else touched. No one but him.

Growing so stiff that he hurt, Rand wondered what set him apart from all the other barbarians in his midst. How could he, a civilized man, be nursing this aching arousal when Sarah's similar plight had brought him here to right this terrible wrong? He didn't know. But his need for Rachel was immense, and he'd never imagined being faced with such raw carnality before assuming his position on the tightrope.

Rand drew in a shuddering, hot breath, tasting spice and the anticipation of woman on his tongue. He commanded himself to raise his gaze again to her face and support her with that until she was his, only his, by virtue of his filthy lucre.

Nonetheless, this atmosphere was bad for a man's morals. And it seduced his to sink lower with each second that passed.

Rachel locked her eyes on Rand. He was the only solid thing she had in the madness that had surrounded her since the minute she'd left the casino with the slaver. She held fast to his presence, to the reassurance she read in his gaze.

But there was more. Something dark and earthy that permeated the room and was focused on her. She shivered and vowed not to cry or scream.

Or dissolve into hysterical laughter. The whole thing was so absurd, so bizarre, she felt as if she were trapped into some B-grade movie and playing the starring role while another part of her observed, in disbelief, from a distance.

Distance. Maurice and company had kept it on the remainder of the flight. Had, in fact, seemed eager to hand her over to this end of the operation that had mercifully proven to be all business. After a staff physician had concurred with the first doctor's findings, she was treated as if she were an investment to be handled with the greatest of care. She'd been bathed, massaged, manicured and pedicured, her hair washed and brushed so that it gleamed like the pennies she'd scrubbed with an eraser as a child until they'd glowed copper-red and new.

Her pubic hair had also been trimmed and fussed over in this exclusive assembly-line for sex slaves in the making. No clothes allowed. She'd counted over thirty naked bodies besides hers, and the treatment of each one was so luxuriantly cavalier that she'd begun to feel oddly liberated by her own nudity. Her ingrained modesty, at home in the Western world, seemed a quaint, outdated custom in this anachronistic, backward society.

For some reason she had been allowed to keep the charm bracelet Rand had given her. The little charms felt like protective talismans against the white silk now binding her wrists while the slight weight of the dangling timepiece helped anchor her to the promise that this would all be over soon. Maybe even five minutes from now it would be over and by this time tomorrow it might even feel like the traces of a disturbing Twilight Zone dream.

An eerie sense of calm enveloped Rachel. The guards departed, leaving her hands bound but unhooked. Maybe it was because of her condescending glare or the lack of struggle which accompanied it. Whatever, it apparently increased her value, judging from the mercenary smile the auctioneer turned on her. The terrible little man pried the wrapped sheet from one breast and then two. The audience *ooohed* and *ahhhed* their beastly approval. The auctioneer winked and she managed not to spit in his face.

Instead, Rachel thrust her breasts out, taking pride in her feminine sculpture. More than pride, she taunted them with it while Rand maintained his outward cool…

Which disintegrated before her stunned eyes.

So attuned to his body talk and the silent support of his gaze, she was struck dumb by his metamorphosis. First, the steady rhythm of his breathing became agitated to the point of panting. Then the clear focus of his eyes on hers lowered to her upper nakedness and became transfixed so that he appeared to be in a trance. His tongue snuck out, tracing a hungry path, around and around as if it were her inner thighs he lapped up rather than his own dry lips.

Her savior was suddenly no savior, and she was horrified to realize that Rand had relinquished his ally's support to stare at her breasts with a hunger unrivaled by his lust-in-the-dust colleagues.

A big gold and ruby studded hook lowered over her head. The auctioneer reached for her wrists.

"I can do it myself you little runt," she hissed, taking her anger out on the nearest scapegoat.

"So you can talk after all," he said in return. "Cooperate and I will not hurt your dignity."

"Go to hell. Dignity's something you don't have to give." Cool air swirled around her breasts and she ignored the agony of feeling more exposed than she had during the two exams. Rachel raised her hands with a grace befitting a ballerina and defiantly notched her chin as she hooked her own wrists above her head, felt the pulley lift her up until she stood on toes that glistened with the red lacquer that had been applied to all her nails.

She shut out the rippling noise of the buyers, the drone of the auctioneer's wheedling voice. If only she could do the same with her hurt, her deep disappointment in Rand, looking at her as if he was more crazed than rest of them. After the time they'd spent together, the bonds they'd forged, how could he turn into this—this *animal*? The fine edge of longing and their unspoken emotions was always like having a third person in the room, but never had she expected their repressed hunger for each other to turn into this kind of betrayal.

It made her want to weep.

She glared at him, at them all, with dragon eyes that were as dry as they were the color of money green. Rand could destroy her illusions of him, and the disgusting men in his ranks could drool all over themselves while she was helpless to cover her near naked-ness, but no one could strip away her pride.

Her body was another matter. Without warning she felt the thin sheet whipped off. An outraged cry ripped from her throat before she could stop it.

"You bastard, get your hands off me!"

"A spirited virgin, gentlemen. And see the lovely hair between her thighs, matching that of her scarlet head."

"Creep! You filthy waste of breathing space—"

"But let us not stop there." He yanked her around and stroked her buttocks.

Gone was her earlier calm. In its place came a flash point rage. With a quick move of self-defense she pulled up and kicked side-ways, landing a solid blow to his groin.

He bent over, groaning and cursing and calling for a whip.

"One hundred thousand American dollars!" came the shout.

"One hundred and fifty!" echoed another.

Voices slashed her ears, dozens of men scrambling to outbid their competition with rubles, yen, pounds and marks.

But why wasn't she hearing Rand through the mayhem while she dangled helpless, naked, and up for grabs?

The auctioneer was quickly gaining his footing, turning her around, gesturing to her breasts, her thighs, then stepping a safe distance away.

"Five hundred thousand American dollars from Prince Dominique," he said triumphantly. "Do I hear a higher bid?"

Rachel stared in shock and fury at Rand. His eyes were glazed; even from here she could see his labored breathing. Was this the same man who had clasped a delicate charm bracelet around the wrist that now burned from a hook and a silk rope? Was this the man who had nearly brought her to her knees while he tried to seduce her agreement not to venture into the very moment of hell that she was now in? No. No, this was a different man—one she no longer recognized even if he was suddenly surging to his feet.

"One million American dollars."

Every head present turned at the commanding sound of his projected voice.

Then silence was followed by murmurs of speculation and respect for the amount of money.

The auctioneer called for silence.

"One million American dollars from the new member. Do I hear more? One million and a half?"

The question was directed to the prince, who remained seated. Rachel held her breath.

The prince, who looked old enough to be her father and had to weigh 300 pounds, nodded. He smiled at her. Then at Rand.

"Two million," Rand countered.

A low ripple from the crowd bespoke their odds-trading on the outcome. This could be a pissing match. Rachel realized she was no longer the only thing here at stake.

Just how much money did Rand have? She couldn't even imagine a million dollars, much less two, and what if the old fat fart had billions to keep outbidding Rand until it came between her and mortgaging everything that he owned?

When the prince shook his head she thought she might collapse from relief.

"The beautiful woman goes for two million!" The delighted auctioneer nodded to Rand. "Come and claim your prize."

She watched as he strode forward, his eyes fluctuating between her face and her naked body. When he gained the stage he stooped and swept up the sheet. He positioned himself between her and the sea of watching eyes, shielding her from every view but his own—and that of the greedy little auctioneer, smiling slyly.

"You will enjoy taming her?"

"I will," Rand said flatly. "But don't ever let me catch you touching her like that again or you'll be looking for another job—along with your hands. Now beat it until we're gone."

As the gnome quickly made his exit, Rand spanned the sheet wide between his arms...and then he just stood there, unmoving, drinking her in. *Why wasn't he covering her up?* The spread of white muslin blended into his fine linen garb, contrasting starkly against his olive skin and making her imagine him as a modern day Valentino. But he was no actor. This was the man she'd spent the last month with, craving his touch, and wondering if she might be falling in love.

Rachel didn't trust herself to speak. She bared her teeth.

The sound he made reminded her of his growl when she'd taught him Daddy's toast. Only this time they weren't in a fancy restaurant with a nearby hoity-toity couple having a spat. They were in an off the map country with an arena of voyeurs straining to get a better view.

Slowly, the highest bidder who had turned into a darker than dark stranger, put the sheet to her back. His hands grazed over her fevered skin, relaying a proprietary feel that spoke of the protection he'd promised but he was hardly providing as she felt him wrap the covering beneath her raised arms only for his fingertips to hover over the top of a breast...

Then slowly close the distance until he touched the tip of a single nipple. His touch became a stroke. Once. Twice. A rolling, gentle squeeze that laced with his tortured groan.

Rachel was appalled to feel both nipples harden and thrust out as if seeking more. Her legs shook and her belly tightened. A tiny, mewling sound escaped between her parted lips to answer his inarticulate murmurings.

Why wasn't she fighting him for all she was worth? She didn't want this, not this way. She abhorred him for what he was doing, for making her acknowledge a shameless facet of herself in this obscene place, making his conquest over her willing body in the privacy of her home seem trivial and pale.

She wanted cling to him. She wanted to bolt and return to a time that was safe and familiar, when she was late with the office rent and had never laid eyes on Rand Slick.

"Mine." The word was a thick whisper and if she hadn't seen his lips move she might have thought she'd imagined it.

Quickly then, as though he didn't trust what he might do next, Rand wrapped the sheet fully around her and secured it between her breasts. She was still dangling from the hook when he pulled her insistently against him.

Even beneath the layers of his clothing she could feel him hard, pulsing. He unhooked her arms and she fell fully against him. Rand caught her so that her bound hands were immobilized between their chests. When she struggled to break away Rand responded with a stern palm fanned over her buttocks, a pelvic lock against his rock hard intentions. His free hand tangled into her hair.

"What are you doing?" she demanded, fighting tears of horror and need.

His mouth came down on hers. Greedily. Possessively. His lips slanted against hers, rubbed them, ate at them as if he was starving for not only her mouth, but every cell in her body, every thought that had ever entered her mind.

Where was her mind? It was nowhere to be found as she was absorbed by a ravenous kiss that made the one they'd finally shared that last night in Vegas seem innocent in comparison. He was making her crazy, yes, she must be losing her mind. Because if only her hands were unbound she would grip him to her, search his back, his chest, delve beneath the clothing he wore to feel him, stroke him, completely know what he was making her own body cry for...

Through her moans, muted by Rand's mouth sucking them up into his own, the faraway rush of rippling applause spread in her ears. The sound cut through and she remembered where she was and with it came the absolute humiliation that she had been ready to beg this man she thought she knew, but clearly didn't know well at all, to take her virginity right here.

Rachel tore her lips from Rand's and reared back. His usually dark shuttered windows were openly dilated pupils and smoking brown logs that were on a barely controlled simmer.

"Let's get out of here and go home," he said hoarsely.

She tried valiantly to keep something of her independence and pushed the words past her kiss swollen lips.

"First you call that ingrate back to give you a knife and cut me loose."

"So you can slap me? The answer is no." Rand hoisted her over his shoulder, one hand locked over the backs of her legs, the other cupping her behind with a possessive caress.

"Stop it," she demanded as the sound of a flute and a sitar blended into the scent of spice and uncurbed desire. "You have no right to do this!"

"The papers that are waiting say that I do."

"You don't own me. I don't belong to you!"

"I guess that's something we'll both have to find out. I just spent a pretty penny to pick up where we left off in Vegas, and judging from this little preview, the answer's going to be worth every dime."

"Put me down!" she shouted. "Do you hear me? Put me down!"

"Better be careful what you ask for, buttercup, because once I put you down, the last thing on your mind will be getting off your back. Trust me."

Trust him? After this, he had to be kidding.

Rachel howled her disgust with him, her shame for her own part in it all, and from what small logic she still had left came the whisper: *What if you were safer with the slavers than you are once he gets you alone?*

The man who had just bought her for a cool two mil gave a smart slap to her squirming behind. And then he paused, took a bow, and gave her a bump on his shoulder before exiting to a standing ovation.

CHAPTER 10

"Dammit, stop! Let me walk!" Rachel hung over Rand's shoulder, smacking his rear with her bound hands since he had the rest of her in a clench. They'd passed through a massive entryway, were bowed to by servants who promptly disappeared, and now he was carrying her up a marbled staircase and through some kind of maze.

She felt him shift, kick, and heard a door slam.

"Did you hear me? I demand that you put me down right this instant!"

"If you say so."

Suddenly she felt herself hauled upright and then he stooped, let go.

She fell a short distance before the softest sensation greeted her back.

Rachel sank into a pillow of clouds. A white canopy that was so huge it might have been a tent was fanned overhead. A quick glance to either side informed her she was laying on a bed, the likes of which she'd never seen before. Round, voluptuous, a gigantic silk pin cushion.

Rand stared down at her. His dark brows were knitted together, making his eyes seem like twin obsidian stones glittering darkly beneath two horizontal slashes.

Rachel couldn't catch her breath and she knew it wasn't from the gentle fall. It was the way he appeared larger than life from her vantage point, dominating the room with his powerful frame dressed in anything but the Wall Street power broker attire she had always seen him in before.

He flung his elaborate skullcap across the room, like he couldn't get rid of it soon enough...and judging from Rand's torched expression, he couldn't wait to get rid of the rest of what he was wearing—along with her sheet while he was at it.

Rachel followed his gaze and realized the sheet she'd been wrapped in had come loose. Her breasts were covered, barely, and so were her hips, even more barely. Her legs were exposed to her upper thighs and sprawled out in a most undignified way.

She pinched them together, only to further loosen the sheet. Her eyes felt like spinning saucers when she felt her breasts completely spill out while the rush of air tickled her feminine parts, only now without the barrier of panties, nylons, or britches.

"Welcome home," he said in a thick voice. "I hope you find our bed comfortable."

"*Our* bed?" Her apprehension soared. Rand was staring at her with even more heated rawness than he had at the auction and was making no effort to disguise what it did for his masculine urges. They tented out from his loose garb like a stern pointer stick aimed directly at her. "The audience is gone, Rand. You can drop the act."

"What makes you think it's an act?"

He sat on the edge of the bed. It gave with his weight and rolled her against him.

"You're a civilized man...aren't you?" she said desperately. "Quit looking at me like that!"

"Like I want to strip off what's left of that sheet in no civilized manner?" he said in a booming, authoritarian tone.

"Stop it," she hissed. "I don't like this. And I don't like you!"

"Actually, I think that you do. You just wish that you didn't," he whispered, then resumed a forceful volume. "Whether you like it or not, makes no difference. We play by my rules, woman, not yours."

"*Your* rules!" She struggled to move away but he caught her upper arms and hoisted her upright until they were almost nose to nose; mouth to mouth. Her rapid, choppy breathing mingled with his, maddeningly deep and even. At least he was no longer panting. Maybe the Rand she knew was still in there somewhere. "Get your hands off me and get out until I'm dressed and you're—"

"I have no intentions of leaving," he bellowed. "Now we're going to do this my way. Give me your hands."

"Why? So you can loop them around a hook and dangle me from the bed while you ravish me?" She heard something that sounded close to hysteria rise in the pitch of her voice.

"Ravish?" The way he said it reminded her of when he repeated 'britches' on her couch and tried not to laugh while he had a finger tickling her crotch. "Don't be ridiculous. When I take you to bed, you'll be more than ready." His words were arrogant but his gaze reflected an array of emotions she was too unstrung to decipher.

Again, he spoke low. "Listen to me, Rachel. You weren't the only one in agony while you were being paraded on that stage. It practically tore my heart out to watch what they did to you."

"Heart?" she repeated. "What heart? The one that had you looking more depraved than all those other sickos combined? The heart that had you all but ransacking my mouth while I was—"

"Giving it back as good as you got?" His grip tightened while his eyes dared her to dispute him.

"Don't be cruel," she whispered. "Don't be someone I wish I'd never met."

"Still the same someone, Angel. There's just a lot more to him than you ever guessed." He raised a brow, and to his credit, if any credit was due at this point, he kept his eyes on hers. "And now something tells me, there's a lot more to Rachel Tinsdale than she ever guessed either, and she's not particularly comfortable with what she's finding out."

It was like she'd had too much to drink and Rand was patting her back over the toilet while he watched from the higher view of one who had learned long ago how to hold his liquor.

"I hate you," she spat, and a part of her really, really did.

"No, you don't." His eyes dipped, warmed, and she could feel her breasts responding with a pert invitation that she hated even more than Rand at the moment. "At least not yet. But you could." Again his eyes engaged hers and she wondered what he saw, causing him to repeat, "You could. And I wouldn't blame you. The wrists?"

"Why should I trust you?"

He pulled up the sheet and covered her breasts, tucked the muslin under her arms, and held out his hands.

Hesitantly, knowing she trusted herself even less than she trusted Rand—*why did he have to put that ugliness into her face?*—she placed her bound wrists into his waiting palms.

For a moment he stared at the bindings as if debating the wisdom of the limited freedom he had offered. Then he lifted her wrists up, placed his lips on the knot, and nuzzled his nose into her open palms. He softly kissed one, then bit gently into the other, before catching her charm bracelet between his teeth and lightly jangling it.

She watched as he let go and began to work the fine knots with fingers that were deft and agile, belying their size and strength. Still too disoriented from the entire ordeal to even try to think beyond her relief that Rand had removed the tether of silk, Rachel studied him because it was sure a heck of a lot easier than studying whatever was going on inside of herself.

"Better?" he asked.

"Better," she confirmed, even knowing she'd never been less better than she had been in her whole entire life.

"None better than you." He rubbed a thumb over an abraded wrist. "The way you've handled yourself is nothing less than amazing. Wish I could say the same."

She nodded her agreement. "Me, too."

Rand actually chuckled. "Hey, great shot on that munchkin. Made me want to whistle and shout, but obviously I was too busy commiserating with the rest of those cretins to be sympathizing with you instead."

"I appreciate you acknowledging that."

"Gotta get what points I can before earning more demerits. Which I no doubt will."

His eyes searched hers and those dark shuttered windows opened enough to confirm he was telling the truth.

"Who *are* you?" she whispered. "Do I know you at all?"

Windows slightly closing. "A little. But you only know what I've wanted you to see. There's a lot more that you haven't." He pressed his forehead to hers and admitted, "I wasn't quite myself at the auction…but then again, maybe I was. There's a lot under the surface that I keep a tight rein on, but when my control slips, it's not pretty. Be careful, Rachel. You haven't seen the worst of me yet."

"Rand?" She pulled away, traced the line of his jaw.

She felt his hands move to her shoulders, then lower to tease, but only tease, the sheet he'd secured at her cleavage. Windows dark and hazy, lowering, then…shut.

"I'll have your bath ordered!" he boomed.

"I can see to my own bath when I'm damn good and ready," she responded quietly. "And I'm not ready yet."

"No?" he said quietly back. "Does that mean you're ready to please your Master?"

A distinctly possessive hand skated up one thigh, then the other before veering straight into the middle. There, he stopped. Rachel could feel the heat of his palm radiating over her pubis. If she lifted her hips even an inch, there would be contact, the kind where there was no going back.

The way his palm continued to hover while his eyes engaged hers in a kind of battle of who would blink first, she was tempted to punish him a little. Ask him if he wanted a closer look at the fine hair that had been washed and clipped with a little bit here, a little bit there, like she was an A list Dorothy in a XXX version of The Wizard of Oz. Just invite him to look and dare him to touch.

Instead, she shook her head, said softly, "No."

"What you mean is, not yet," he corrected.

It was going to happen. She knew it. He knew it. They both did. The only question was when and what her terms would be. For all of Rand's awful behavior, for all of his huffing and puffing, in her heart of hearts she knew that he would never take her unless she invited his taking. Anything less would rob King Kong of his ultimate prowess over the woman who they both knew was calling the shots until she willingly gave in.

"Fine!" she shouted when he crooked his ridiculously handsome head towards the door. "Fine! I'll take a bath. Just don't come back until next year. I should be real clean by then."

Rand grinned.

"So the auctioneer didn't lie," he retorted with a little pat to her not-so-private anymore privates, a gesture that felt unexpectedly affectionate, like she was a new puppy and he couldn't resist a parting stroke to her fur. "You are a spirited wench! Now get this, my virgin possession. I will return when it suits me and you would be wise to curb your tongue when I do."

He winked. And then he flapped a sheet over her exposed

parts before striding away from the bed. *Why*, she wondered, *why* did he always have to go and do something decent after proving what an ass he could be? A Rubik's Cube. No kidding. And she'd have to be ten times crazy not to steer clear of those missing parts and rusted hinges that she'd first glimpsed when he whipped a pen out of her hand and threw it to her office desk—all because she'd asked, *"And just who are you, Mr. Slick?"*

Well. At least he'd tried to be honest with her this time. She could give him a point or two for that. Rachel just wished it wasn't so hard to remain on the bed where she was safe for now, instead of so wanting to go after him and find out his secrets, what had happened to make him this way.

Rand threw open the ornately carved Master's Chambers door. Rachel heard the sound of retreating footsteps hurrying down the hallway, followed by his shout in that direction.

"Jayna!"

More scrambling back.

"Yes, Master?"

Rachel could just make out the figure of an older woman cloaked from head to toe in black, bowing near the open door.

"Take proper care of this woman. *MY* woman. If she gives you any trouble tell me and I will deal with her."

"Yes, Master."

Then Rand was gone.

The elderly woman he left her with, Jayna, who was to be her guard and apparently a great masseuse as well, looked Rachel up and down with a seasoned eye.

Rachel didn't get the immediate feeling that Jayna was all that impressed.

"I will draw your bath," Jayna informed her new charge.

Although Rachel wasn't Catholic this Jayna sounded a lot like the Sister-in-Charge from Hell—the one who wouldn't hesitate to rap your knuckles hard as she could, only to put the ruler behind her back and turn a sweet smile on the parish priest.

Rachel knew she'd test the bath water before she got in, make sure her tush didn't end up redder than her hair.

There was one other thing she knew: Someway, somehow, she needed to make scary Jayna her new best friend.

Jayna would be key to getting Sarah out of the bathhouse.

CHAPTER 11

R and shut the door to his office. It was arranged to be almost an exact duplicate of the one he kept in New York, complete with a revolving bookcase that hid an adjacent private study and sound proofed sleeping area. The entire top two floors of a Manhattan sky rise were his and the people occupying those floors answered to him. And just as with this office, he preferred a smaller space to consolidate his maneuvers rather than claiming the biggest swath of corner windows to flash his position as a "Big Swinging Dick"—the most coveted title in finance among the major traders on The Street.

But real power, he had learned, was stealthy. Understated. Ego swaggered around; the real power brokers, you never saw them coming.

Rachel had real power—over him. They both knew it. And she had not abused that knowledge…at least, not yet.

Trust was not a commodity he was overly familiar with. Rachel was, quite possibly, the only person he had truly trusted since being deserted by a bum who had left him with a wrinkled five dollar bill that could have been filched out of a pocket or a sewer for all he knew. But the intent had been kind, and even if transient, it had stuck with him.

Rand gently placed Rachel's white silk rope on his desk. A Persian rug muffled his short trek to the bookcase. The contents couldn't have been more different from one that held a silver flask, can of mace, and a one-eyed Raggedy Ann doll. Scanning several of his favorite titles—*Liar's Poker* by Michael Lewis; *Den of Thieves*, James B. Stewart; *Barbarians At The Gate*, Burrough and Helyar—he removed *Liar's Poker*, butted up against the frame. Two precisely placed holes, only the size of a fingertip, accessed an internal lever —similar to a light switch for off and on, except for open and close. Simple. Effective. Discreet.

The bookcase swung open and he entered a small handsome study. There, Rand took off the local costume that made him want to crawl into the tub with Rachel and get real clean himself. He was tempted to take a shower but that meant he'd lose the lingering scent of the bare flesh he had openly handled in public, and he knew it wasn't just for show.

It was disturbing to think of how he may as well have raised his leg and pissed all over the stage to mark his territory. The urge was still there, like a low, jungle drum beat that was tracking the quickening pace of their shifting relationship. He could feel it—the want, the ever-present need to breathe her in and eat her up; but there was a new depth to his urgency and a finer edge to his fear that if he exposed too much of himself Rachel would have the good sense to act on self-preservation.

And if she did?

At one time he would have pulled out every trick in his little black book to mess with her good sense. Now it was like the Big Swinging Dick tycoon he had invented was getting elbowed around by a horny, lovesick sap with a conscience. Rachel wanted to know who he was? So much of his life was a lie he didn't even know where to start...

Actually, he did.

"What's your name, son?"

"Rand Slick."

Only a kid who'd inhaled too many gumshoe novels from a Woolworths' spinning book rack would have come up with such a name—then spent over twenty years perfecting a persona that could live up to such a ridiculous invention.

Rand swung open the doors to a masculine teak wardrobe that housed the clothes he had become most comfortable wearing. There were no khakis, no jeans, no boat shoes or chambray shirts. Suits, all custom made. Shirts, all pristine white and the best money could buy, with the initials **RS** discreetly embroidered in black on the cuffs. Shoes, Allen Edmonds, size 12, and yes it was an indicator, but they'd get that worked out if it proved to be an issue.

As for the Allen Edmonds, his choice of shoes was as deliberate as the rest of his outward crafting. Every President since Reagan took office in 1981 had worn them.

The shoes helped him feel a little more grounded as he swung the bookcase back to conceal his private quarters, hit the lock, and returned *Liar's Poker* to its designated place on the shelf.

Settling behind his desk in the dressed-for-success disguise no one had ever disputed, unless he counted himself, Rand wondered if some of the highest power brokers in the world had ever wrestled with as many quandaries as he did now.

"And best of all, she is a virgin!"

Had he ever been a virgin? He supposed, only to leave that virginity behind the moment he'd climbed out of Sarah's window. His sexual virginity was more of a transaction for the need of money than fulfilling his first "benefactor's" fantasy of being something her much older husband couldn't provide. He'd lied then too, saying he was nineteen instead of the sixteen he was, but hey, what sixteen-year-old boy wouldn't count it his luckiest day ever to get paid to let the equivalent of a really hot aunt romp all over him and teach him what she was missing in bed?

Rand tried to focus on some spread sheets. He straightened the silk Brioni tie he'd bought on his last trip to Italy.

And all he could see was the white binding he'd removed from Rachel's wrists that now resided next to a tiny bottle of *Tweed* on his executive's desk. Eames. An original. Nothing like the 50's schoolhouse throwback in the office that was just as original as Rachel, where he'd first gotten high on her strangely familiar but elusive scent.

Maybe he could help make up for what he'd done at the auction by giving her this one small gift that he hadn't wanted to relinquish since claiming it from the dumpster where Jack had put him on notice.

Rachel had put him on notice that same night. It troubled him a bit, more than a bit, that his quest to get Sarah out of here was already running into the emotional interference Rachel had warned him about. They'd only taken up residence together today and yet here he was fully aware that he didn't want to leave until he was convinced that Rachel wouldn't bolt once they were out of a country where he legally owned her.

No, he wasn't above borrowing time…even at Sarah's expense.

God, he was such a selfish bastard.

Rachel would find out soon enough if she didn't guess it already. But tonight, which was expected to be the official night of consummation followed by a barbaric ritual of public evidence, he would prove that even a bad penny like him might be worth something.

This was his palace. His domain. He pocketed the white silk. Took a quick sniff from the little *Tweed* bottle; pocketed that.

Rand left his useless executive Eames desk to head for the gourmet kitchen where he would execute orders for a memorable dinner, and leave with more than he arrived with.

He hoped Rachel was enjoying her bath and Jayna's ministrations since, selfish bastard that he was, he had no intentions of leaving Zebedique until he was certain that Sarah wasn't the only girl who'd ever looked at him as if he'd hung the moon and could swing her on a star.

Under Jayna's watchful eye, Rachel entered the bathing area. By no stretch of the imagination could she just call it a bathroom since it was as over-the-top voluptuous as the Master's Chambers that opened into it via double doors.

No lock. She'd checked.

There was no shower. But the sunken tub with water spouting out of a dolphin's gold mouth—24karat was her guess—could easily accommodate four.

"Looks like I can take some laps in there if I need more exercise than what I got bought for today."

Jayna said nothing but Rachel thought she detected a glimmer of sympathy from elderly eyes. It made her wonder if Jayna had once been in a similar position, just not as staged as her own.

"What makes you think I'm acting?" Rand had asked.

The way he'd manhandled her on the stage, then gotten into his role once he dropped her on *"our bed,"* had her insides still quivering. It bothered her to acknowledge some of that quiver was from imagining more of that manhandling as he staked ownership rights in a not-so-pretend kind of way.

"Nice toilet," she said, trying to make conversation. Pointing to a matching oblong bowl minus a tank and a lid, but sporting two gold handles shaped like swans, she asked, "What's that?"

"You do not know?"

"Nope."

Jayna raised a finely arched eyebrow, cocked her head, and

that's when Rachel noticed she had a bead of sweat trickling past the heavy black scarf covering her head.

"It is a bidet." She demonstrated how the swan handles pushed water up from the middle of the bowl. "You sit upon it facing the handles and clean yourself. You will use it more than the toilet."

"Oh." Oh, indeed. "Hey, even nearly naked, I'm really warm in here. You've got to be burning up under all those clothes. Why don't you take off your head thing, at least while we're alone?"

Jayna looked shocked. Had she stepped over a cultural line and erased any progress she might have made with still-a-little-bit scary Jayna?

"Of course you could just go cool off in the, um, Master's Chambers," Rachel hastened to add. "Maybe read a book or something while I take a few laps and try out that bidet."

"It is not permitted." Jayna shook her head firmly, but Rachel caught her longing glance towards the relative coolness of the adjoining chambers. "You have much to learn."

"And I'll be real appreciative for what you can teach me, Jayna. But there's no reason you have to stay uncomfortable while you do. I don't want you sweating because of me. I'm not here because I want to be..." That wasn't completely true, but the rest of what she said was. "And chances are, neither are you. So why don't we make a deal that'd be good for us both?"

If there was such a thing as wary, she was looking at it now. At least if Jayna decided to rat on her, she wasn't worried about any forthcoming wrath from Rand.

Rachel pushed her case in Jayna's continued silence.

"Listen, if we're both stuck here with you having the job of looking after me, the least I can do is look after you, too. Girl power! The master doesn't have to know if we're playing cards or looking at magazines when he's not around. No reason for us to be bored while he's doing...whatever he's doing when he's not jumping my bones."

"Cards? Magazines?" Jayna shook her head as if she'd just stepped into an alternate reality and was trying to wake up. "Where would you get such things?"

Rachel knew exactly where she would get them. She just wasn't saying beyond a conspiratorial smile.

"I can teach you how to play Poker but maybe we'll start with Rummy since it's better for two players."

Jayna averted her eyes, approached the sunken tub where steam was rising. She shut off one golden knob, left the other one going. Rachel was laying odds it was cold water that continued to stream into the tub.

"The custom is to have the water as hot as possible to wash away any past knowledge of another man from your body. I do not think your body has had such knowledge before."

Boy, was this Jayna smart.

"Yep," Rachel confirmed. "I'm a bona fide virgin. Seems that made me some pretty pricey goods today."

"Such goods should be used wisely." Jayna smiled, hesitated, then took her headdress off, carefully laid it aside, and picked up a waiting towel. She patted her sweating forehead, shook out a magnificent mane of salt-and-pepper hair.

What Rachel saw was a woman who had been beautiful once. And Jayna was looking back at her as if imagining she was young again too, before life had taken its toll and reduced her to drawing a much needed paycheck for the kind of work she knew everything about and wished she didn't.

Rachel removed the sheet as Jayna poured exotically scented oil into the water and gestured for her to enter the tub. It smelled like Pier One had turned into pure liquid surrounding her in silken warmth. Not too hot. Not too cold. Her tush might end up a little pink, but pleasantly so.

She wished that Jayna could enjoy such luxury. And so she said.

Jayna's laugh was soft. "That is very kind of you, Mistress."

"Call me Rachel."

"If you wish, but only when the master cannot hear. You would be wise to obey him," Jayna advised. "Even wiser to please him and gain his favor. He is your Master but he is also a man, no? Even a bed slave might have power over a man."

And with that sage bit of advice, Rachel knew that Jayna could be her ally. She just couldn't get too ambitious, too soon, about getting Jayna on board. Jayna had too much to lose if anything went wrong and for now it was all about securing trust.

"Guess I'm lucky since this new master of mine's not exactly bad looking. Way better than that Prince Dominique who tried to outbid him and could flatten me like a pancake with his big belly."

"Prince Dominique?" Jayna grimaced and wrung a sea sponge with a tight fist before putting it to Rachel's back. "You were spared. Be grateful."

It was then that Rachel fully realized how much she had taken for granted when paying the office rent was her biggest worry and Rand Slick had yet to open her door. Funny how a single moment, a single meeting could change your entire life in so little time—

Time. The timepiece on her charm bracelet! She'd been so careful not to get it wet during all the ministrations preceding the auction. Had she ruined it?

She lifted her left wrist, shook it out. The charms jangled on either side of the tiny watch that she put to her ear.

Tick. Tick. Tick.

Whew. Apparently Rand's gift from Tiffany's was waterproof, too.

"What are these?" Jayna asked, nodding at the little charms.

"I'm not sure what they all mean, but somebody special gave the bracelet to me, and maybe one day I'll find out."

They looked like player's pieces from a Monopoly board: A train, a thimble, a racecar, a shoe. There was also the dangling likeness of a doll, a little house, a globe, and a card—the Queen of Hearts.

"Much can be revealed in time. Perhaps you might even teach me to play cards one day—and I will teach you other things in exchange."

"Sure works for me. I'll find a way to get those cards and teach you how to shuffle tomorrow."

"You think to play cards with me tomorrow? It is not likely."

"How come?"

Jayna slid her a look that said she must not be the sharpest crayon in the box.

"The Master. He is young and strong. Even a week from now you may not have emerged from these chambers. Prepare yourself."

"But isn't there a bathhouse or someplace I'm supposed to go to on Fridays?"

The loofa on her back stilled. "How would you know of the bathhouse?"

Rachel quickly splashed some water onto her face, hoping Jayna didn't see her "oops" look of chagrin. *Dammit.* The only reason she knew about the bathhouse was because of Rand.

"When the slavers had me corralled with those other bed slaves we got a lot of pampering from some local ladies who told us about Fridays being girl's day out and they looked forward to seeing us again at the bathhouse."

Jayna resumed her back scrubbing. "I see. And did they tell you that you may not enter if you are unclean?"

"Excuse me?"

That look again. Maybe Rand could get her a pencil sharpener to go with some magazines and cards.

"If it is your time to bleed, you are not allowed to be seen in public—or to soil the water for the other slaves who are there to relax and wash their master's touch from their bodies."

Oh. Shit. Her ability to get to Sarah had just been cut in half—unless they were on the same cycle, and there was a whopping 25 percent chance of that.

"Guess they never heard of tampons around here, huh?"

Jayna's expression confirmed it. Great. Just great. Now if they were still here when that time rolled around—a little over two weeks—she'd have to ask Rand to somehow import her some necessities. *Had he known about any of this stuff and decided not to tell her?* She wouldn't put it past him.

"It is time." Jayna rose, handed Rachel a luxurious, warm towel. The kind that Jackie O or the Queen of England might use. "The others will take over. I wish you luck."

A small encouraging smile and Jayna made to leave.

"Jayna, wait!"

"Yes?"

"What happens next? What am I supposed to do now?"

Jayna shrugged. "My assistants will come in and prepare your hair, paint your mouth with berry juice, line your eyes with kohl. You will be dressed in the fine gown the master has selected. You will be beautiful and waiting for your master."

Gulp. "Anything else I should know?"

Jayna patted pursed lips as if trying to find the right way to put this. "Yes. Yes, there is something else you should prepare for. There is a custom. It is like a parade. All the masters hang sheets outside to show what they paid for. The sheet you will share with your master tonight will be outside your balcony by the time the sun rises."

CHAPTER 12

*R*and paused outside the Master's Chambers door. Listening, he heard nothing of Rachel's movements. Of course she just might be standing inches away, ready to clobber him with a pillow if she was still pissed about any of his earlier behavior.

Their kiss-but-not-kiss-and-make-up session post auction had stuck with him like a sweet lump of sugar wedged into the back of his throat. After he'd taken care of business in the kitchen, that sweet lump had induced him to venture to the marketplace where he'd made a carefully considered purchase. The time wasn't right to present that particular gift, but he did have the bottle of *Tweed*, along with another filled vial, waiting in a pocket of his raw silk trousers. Appropriately black, as was the matching embroidered Zebedique version of a smoking jacket.

His hand was poised to knock—but then he remembered his role and went directly for the knob.

His breath left him. She was facing the window, looking out to the indigo sky, her hand clenched into voluminous drapes. White gauze spilled through her ruby painted nails and trailed the ground, blending into the delicate gown he had personally selected and she now wore. One shoulder was bare, the other half covered by flowing, sheer fabric. Rachel's back was partially exposed, revealing skin as rich and soft as cream icing on a cake. It contrasted with the cascade of her hair—a study in scarlet temptation.

He wondered if she was trying to drive him crazy.

Rand firmly shut the door and saw her give a small start before whirling around to face him.

Holy hell, forget crazy, she was locking him up and throwing away the key.

Rand cleared his throat since swallowing wasn't possible with his mouth so dry. "I see you've adapted something of a local touch."

"Do you like it?" Her voice was unsure, anxious perhaps.

"I don't know if *like* is the word." He advanced and her kohl lined eyes darted to the bed.

"The cosmetics are a lot different here than what I use at home. Maybe I should wash it off."

"Absolutely not." He stopped maybe a foot away, maintaining enough distance to drink the whole of her in yet still close enough to reach out and touch the penciled in beauty mark riding the sweet curve of her cheek. "You are a goddess."

She gave him a return once-over and he could feel his blood rush from no more than the appreciative sweep of her gaze. "You're not too shabby yourself. That outfit goes perfect with those one-way windows of yours."

"One-way windows?"

"Your eyes, Rand. Most of the time you're looking out but nobody else can look in. Every now and then, even if it's just a crack, I try to peek in before you know I'm looking."

"I always know when you look." And he did. Somehow he had to start letting let her look more often, even when the interior grew dark. "What do you see now?"

"Hard to tell when those windows get so steamy."

"Steamy windows should tell you plenty." He caught her chin, kept the windows open. "Worried about tonight?"

"Should I be?"

He lowered his gaze to her luscious lips but denied himself more than that. "You tell me, Angel."

Rachel took a small step back. She put a palm against his chest, left it there, and he wondered if she could feel the pump of his heart. It beat too hard, too fast. It beat for her.

"Jayna told me some things that I wasn't expecting to hear, and I have to wonder if you held out on me."

Of course he had, but instead he asked, "And just what might those things be?"

"For starters, I'm apparently not allowed into the bathhouse during a certain time of the month—which could extend our stay here if I can't hook up with Sarah in the next two weeks."

"Oh, yes. That. I brought some items you might want that aren't freely available here, just in case."

Her blush deepened. "How thoughtful of you."

He'd thought so. What he hadn't expected was for his first venture into the feminine hygiene section of Walgreens to feel like such an oddly intimate experience. Of course being Vegas even Walgreens blared a neon welcome.

"I wasn't sure what to get, so you should have plenty to choose from even if we're here for the next year."

"The next year?" She smacked his chest. "The next year!"

"Just kidding."

"That's not funny, Rand."

"Sorry," he lied, and brought her hand to his lips for a conciliatory kiss to the knuckles she probably wanted to plant into his sternum. "Anything else Jayna told you that might be of a more immediate concern?"

Rachel narrowed her kohl lined eyes straight into the windows he forced himself not to shut.

"So, you knew about what's supposed to happen tonight, too, didn't you? With the sheet and letting everybody on the street gawk at it in the morning."

"Oh. That. Yes, I knew." He thought about alleviating her indignant concern with the ultimate gift he had brought her, but instead reached into his pocket and held out the little bottle of *Tweed*. "Maybe you'll forgive me for that oversight and dab a little of this behind your ears. Or, wherever else you might be inclined to entice me for a closer nuzzle."

"Where did you get this?" She snatched the bottle from his outreached palm and held it to her as if he'd returned an entire treasure chest from the bottom of an ocean.

"The dumpster, where they tossed everything but you and your dress." Just remembering made his jaw clench while his insides felt like swamp water.

"I can't believe you went dumpster diving."

How little she still knew about him.

"Wasn't the first time." It was a very generous and painful admission on his part, even if Rachel didn't seem to comprehend more than her delight over having the small bottle of perfume unexpectedly returned.

"I put it into my purse at the last minute. After...after what happened between us before we left for the casino. It was like the bracelet you gave me. I knew I might not see either of them again but I needed to take some lucky charms with me."

"I'm glad they let you keep one. And now you have both."

"Jayna asked me what the charms meant."

"And what did you tell her?"

"That I wasn't sure. That someone special had given the bracelet to me, and I hoped that one day that someone might tell me if the charms had a special meaning. Do they?"

"If you have to ask then maybe you don't know me as well as I had hoped despite my tendency to withhold information when that seems the wiser course to take."

Rachel considered the charms, one by one.

"Want to tell me now?"

"No." Rand turned away. He had let her in, but he was still stingy with how much he gave up because once given, there was no taking it back. What Rachel couldn't know was that they were skirting some very private territory that made a consummation sheet hanging outside seem relatively modest compared to the interior workings she was digging into—which he had invited the minute he gave her the bracelet.

"When?"

Rand stared at ruby painted nails gripping his arm, pulling him back and closer to the danger Rachel posed. His was a carefully constructed life made up of secrets and lies he kept as closely guarded as a junkyard protected by a really mean pit bull.

He was owner of that junkyard. He was the pit bull. One that was hard pressed to stay very mean every time he looked at her; every time she looked at him; every time they touched.

His gaze settled on the shoe dangling from her bracelet.

"Dinner should be ready soon. Would you care for a tour before I ply you with some very fine libations and the best our kitchen has to offer?"

Rachel shook the bracelet and pointed to the door. "Fine! Be that way, Mr. Smoke and Mirrors. I'll get to the bottom of you yet."

"Just work your way down from the top and take your time doing it." He puckered his lips. "A kiss before we go?"

"You're impossible!" Rachel flounced to the ornately carved Master's Chambers door and reached for the handle.

Before she could throw the door open he pushed it back, palm pressed firmly against wood, his body closing in. His eyes met hers. Suddenly they were no longer in Zebedique, in the palace where he supposedly owned her, but right where they'd left off against her door in Vegas when he'd tried to seduce her agreement not to be exactly where they were now.

"I am impossible," he agreed. "And you're impossibly delicious. I could easily call for room service instead of having dinner downstairs where we have to be a lot more careful about what we discuss. Anything else, just between us two, if you'd rather get out of here while I'm still offering the option?"

Rachel looked torn between tearing off his clothes and keeping her own on.

"I'm making friends with Jayna. We need her. And I need you to get me some cards, along with some magazines."

"Magazines?"

"Yeah. Cosmo. Better Homes and Gardens. Mechanics Illustrated. Doesn't matter. They'll all be new to her and give us something to talk about besides bidets and a period making a woman unclean." Rachel visibly cringed. "So embarrassing. Me and my dad never had those discussions and I'm not exactly comfortable discussing Mother Nature with you."

"I understand. I never had those talks either." He hesitated—then bit the bullet. "Like you, I had a good father, at least for a while, but dads don't necessarily make good mothers, even if they try to cover both bases. My mother died when Sarah was born, and I know my dad loved us but he had trouble showing affection. I think that's where mothers come in—a kiss on a scraped knee, a hug just because. Kids need nurturing to grow up healthy and right. I could have used a lot more of it." He paused, went for it. "I've never been in a committed relationship before. I don't have much experience with affection, with trust, or actual intimacy, so I do appreciate your patience with me—it has been noted. You should also know that I always sleep alone. Nightmares."

Vulnerability didn't even begin to describe the degree of exposure he felt. It was actually a little hard to breathe and the urge was great to race away and gasp what oxygen he could from the free air on the street that would support his ever running feet.

She stayed him with eyes soft and steady on his, followed by a simple, "Thank you, Rand. I'll take good care of that information."

Whew. She hadn't asked for more than he was willing to divulge and in the wake of his difficult bit of gut spilling, he felt something close to relief.

Rand crooked his arm. "Tour before dinner?"

"If the master's offering, I'm not turning him down."

Rachel latched onto his elbow with a little snicker.

"What's so funny?"

"According to Jayna even a love slave might master the man who bought her and I'd be smart to please you."

"Jayna deserves an immediate raise."

"Be extra nice to her, Rand. Jayna's our ticket to Sarah."

Rand considered how he was secretly in no hurry to get Rachel into the bathhouse, even knowing that for every second he indulged himself, his sister could be paying a pretty price for it.

He was making progress, but the baby steps he was taking wouldn't cover much distance without an extended amount of time. He needed to step up his efforts.

Hopefully Rachel was ready for a bumpy thrill ride on a dark desert highway. Seatbelt or no seatbelt, he was hitting the gas.

Rachel studied her dining companion across the table that could pass for a bowling lane with him at one end and her at the other—though who was throwing the ball and who was positioned to fly like ten pins, she wasn't sure. Ever since Rand had told her more about his childhood and certain issues in the adult department, the atmosphere between them had changed. Exactly how, she couldn't say, but something was happening. Or was about to.

It felt dangerous. And dangerously exciting.

Did guys ever get butterflies in their stomachs? Or was that just a girl thing? Maybe she'd ask him.

Rachel cupped her palms around the mouth that could really go for a kiss and called, "Hellooo down there! Do guys ever get butterflies in their tummies?"

The goblet he'd just put to his lips came back down on the table. She wasn't sure since he moved his head but she thought he'd just spewed.

After patting his mouth with a big linen napkin—why was *everything* so BIG around here?—he surged from the chair that resembled a throne and struck a powerful pose.

Oooh. Definitely big everything.

"Woman!" he bellowed. "Your impertinence will not be tolerated! You will leave your chair now and come to your master for a suitable chastisement."

She thought about taunting him with a "Make me," only they did have their roles to play and maybe getting chastised by Rand wouldn't be such a bad thing.

Pretending outrage, she rose from her chair with a loud huff... and proceeded to strut like a burlesque queen his way, swinging the swath of white gauze that was draped over her shoulder as if it were a pastie tassel for some mega knockers.

She loved the way his eyes were eating her up and she thrilled to the way her teasing walk held a captive audience that looked ready to drop to his knees.

"Yes, Master?"

Rand gripped the light fabric she'd been swinging and yanked it, along with her, against him.

"Oh Rachel," he whispered, "You give me far too much credit if you think there will not be retribution for pulling something like that."

"You didn't answer me," she whispered back. "Do guys get butterflies in their tummies? Or, I guess, more to the point—do you?"

"Only when you're around. But my butterflies have a way of migrating south."

He gave her a meaningful bump.

"I'm not hungry," she confessed.

"I am." He put his lips to her neck, skated up, and into her ear came his breath. "For you."

She was ready. Past ready. The energy it was taking to deny the inevitable made her PI's cardinal rule seem like cutting off her nose to spite her face—or maybe that's just what she was telling herself to justify her decision: If there was going to be a consummation sheet hung from the balcony, let it fly.

"Then maybe we should get ourselves back to the Master's Chambers," she suggested. "Should you haul me over your shoulder again while I make all the suitable noises of protest?"

In answer he did haul her over his shoulder, locked one arm behind her knees, grabbed an open bottle of wine from the table, and pounded up the marbled staircase while she screamed, "No! No! You're a monster! A beast!"

"And now you will find out just what a beast I can be!"

There was a lack of theatrics to his tone that made her wonder if he was being as sincere as with his earlier confession. This place, this Zebedique, was changing them somehow. In the free world she had her office, he had his; they could come and go as they pleased, but here? All they really had were each other and the absolute trust it took to work together as a team.

As he kicked the door shut to ensconce them into the grand domain of the bedchamber, Rachel knew the britches she'd kept up were finally going down. *Good riddance.* As for Rand always sleeping alone, they'd just see about that.

Especially when the room was lit with what had to be a hundred candles. Moonlight threaded between fluttering drapes with an exotic scented wind whispering through slightly open balcony doors.

Oh yeah. If a girl was going to lose her virginity, this was definitely the way to do it.

He deposited her beside the silk pin cushioned bed.

Rand sat on the edge, placed the wine bottle on the floor, and patted the space beside him. "Sit with me."

It wasn't what she had expected. Then again, when had he ever done anything she expected?

Rachel sat. Rand looked off into the distance.

"Aren't you supposed to be pouring us some wine and getting me loose to claim your masterly rights?" she finally asked when the silence lengthened. "I mean, we have this sheet thing to take care of and…and I know you'll make it good for me, and ever since you walked into my office we've known that we'd end up in bed together." She gave a little bounce. "This one seems pretty comfy. Better than my mattress at home. Better than the wall there, too."

Rand looked at her, windows wide open, and Hotel California didn't even come close to what she saw.

He shook his head. "That's not how this is going down. Not tonight anyway. What happens between us is just between us, nobody else. We'll give them what they're expecting, but on our terms."

He rose from the bed, pulling her with him. "I want you to do this with me."

"Do what?" she asked.

"Help me with the ceremonial sheet."

Rand whipped the prepared sheet off the mattress, handed her one end and proceeded to flap out the other. She flapped, too. Then he bent, so did she, and the sheet glided to the floor, illuminated by candles and the filtered light of the moon.

"What now?"

He removed his embroidered jacket, exposing his chest to her for the first time, and…*Oh. Ohhh.* No man had any right to look that fine unless he was benching two hundred pounds and training for the Olympics.

"Now meet me in the middle." He extended his hand, like he was asking her to dance.

As she accepted his invitation, he withdrew a small vial from a pocket that rode a hip of his impressively tented lounge pants.

"What's this?"

"A gift from the kitchen." He gave a short bow, placed the vial into her palm. "A gift from me to you. Open it."

Rachel uncorked it. The faint tinny smell of blood infiltrated her nostrils while the scent of Rand, so close and nearly naked but not nearly naked enough bore in. His smile was almost benevolent, though benevolence was the last thing she wanted when a ski team could slalom down her inner thighs.

"And now?"

"Now you kiss me"—he leaned in, whisper close—"and you pour."

As his lips met hers, Rachel dropped the vial to let it land where it may.

She gripped him to her and urged him down to the sheet they had spread together onto the floor.

For being such a big bad wolf, Rand Slick was surprisingly sweet. Maybe even a little too sweet, given the fact she was mostly the aggressor who was improvising as she went and he was clearly liking it, judging from his enthusiastic response that made her feel like an A student in chemistry—

Until he made it suddenly clear that she was, indeed, in the presence of a master.

"Don't you want to feel me?" He urged her hand from his chest lower, lower, a dip beneath the fabric riding his hips. "Believe it or not, I'm not so easy myself these days. I've been celibate for the past year, unless you count your couch, your door, and a lot of quality alone time since you put a gun in my face and started blowing me away. Do you ever think about me and—"

His sharp intake of breath coincided with her sudden grip of his phallus. His skin was so smooth, the organ it covered an astounding work of nature that pulsed in her hand—or as much as she could get around it. Her fingers couldn't quite meet around the circumference at the base...but sliding up, it was like learning the sculpture of a lighthouse that narrowed and ended with a plump beacon on top.

"You're beautiful." Now that she had him, she wanted more, wanted to see what she could do to him, if there really was power to be had over a man who certainly had plenty of power over her.

What he was doing to her breasts while she stroked him made her wonder if a woman could orgasm from the sensation of cool air and moisture, alternate suckles and flicks of a warm, seeking tongue. His hands were elsewhere, leisurely disrobing her and taking far too long to get rid of it all. She was tempted to help him out but that would mean letting go of what she'd latched onto and wasn't about to give up until he put it where it belonged.

"Make love to me." It wasn't a request; this was urgent, a demand. "Make the blood on the sheet for real."

Rand went suddenly still. He gripped her pumping wrist.

"Not tonight. Those bastards don't get that from us. We'll cheat..." He released her wrist and slid a warm palm over the apex of her thighs...then delved, began to circle her cleft with a thumb that felt like he loved her there, loved her everywhere, and was in no hurry to leave, if ever. "You feel like heaven, Angel, and believe me I'm in some kind of hell to draw this line. I'll make love to you, but no penetration. I won't have any blood of yours on public view. It's the principle of the thing."

Well who knew? Rand Slick had more principles than her.

She had wondered if she was falling in love with her first big client. She still wondered if he might break her heart after the job was done and the danger, the adventure, the adrenaline that he gravitated to would still be in New York, while she would be returned to a very different life 2500 miles away.

At the moment she didn't care. Maybe Rand would break her heart once they were back in reality, but for now she had an epic erection in her hand that he was refusing to deflower her with. *Dammit.*

"About that cheating…" She raised her hips, encouraging him to reconsider.

"Mmm. Yes."

"Maybe we could compromise on the penetration part?"

"You know, Ms. Tinsdale, you've always been a bit of a challenge and compromise has never been one of my strong suits. But let's see what we can work out."

And he entered her. Only a testing finger, then two not so testing, and the way he played her interior flesh, plumbing right down to her soul, had her writhing all over the sheet along with the vial she'd dropped that could be staining her skin even now. And all the while she refused to let go of his magnificent erection that was all her doing, and if that wasn't power, she didn't know what was.

He brought her to a climax that felt like she'd barreled into a head-on collision and went straight through the windshields of his eyes, openly watching her in the throes of a seemingly endless orgasm—

That was not hers alone.

The spurt of hot liquid filled her palm and kept filling it to overflowing, and now she watched him, his face a study of what could have been rapture or pain in the flickering candlelight, his eyes tightly closing, his breath coming in quick, sharp pants like that of a marathon runner.

And when he opened his eyes again, when he removed the fingers that were inside her, when he kissed them then reached for the hand he had filled, sealing their fluids between locked palms, Rachel fully realized how much trouble she was in.

She wasn't just in love with Rand Slick. She was desperately and completely out of her mind in love with a man who was laying his imperfect cards on the table.

"I'll deal with the sheet and stay until you're asleep. When you wake up, I'll be gone. I'm not sure if, or when, that will ever change. I'm a man with closely held secrets, Rachel. I have a past that I've carefully buried and you really don't want to dig up. But none of that changes the fact that what I feel for you is something extraordinary. If I ever give you cause to doubt me, and I could, please never doubt how deeply you move me."

CHAPTER 13

When Rachel woke up it was to the sound of cheering outside. Dappled sunlight played through fluttering curtains. No sheet on the floor. No candles still burning.

No Rand. He'd kept his promise. He wasn't here.

She knew what the cheering was about and allowed herself a smug smile while pulling the covers up closer around her. Rand had been right to draw the line and impose the discipline she had wanted him to ditch.

Besides. Last night was by far the most mind-blowing "everything but" she'd ever had. And now they had a secret.

She touched her neck and could still feel his lingering suckle. No doubt she had a whopper of a hickey...or maybe just several smaller ones around the same area. Sometimes he surprised her by how discreet he could be.

But then again...

Any man with a carefully buried past, who was carrying around some loaded secrets, wasn't going to be dancing on tables or swinging from chandeliers.

She wondered if he would regret telling her as much as he had.

If he might even instinctively pull back. Well, just let him try. She wasn't giving up an inch of the ground he'd finally given her—and she wouldn't hesitate to use whatever it took to keep him coming back for more.

A light tap sounded at the door and her heart gave a little jump —then dropped. Rand would just barge in, being the master and all that.

"Come in," she called.

"Good afternoon, Mistress." Jayna rolled in a serving cart.

"It's afternoon already?"

"Yes. The master requested that I bring you lunch. He said..."

"Yes?" Rachel asked, trying not to sound too eager, while her eyes lighted on what was definitely a prettily wrapped package beside a delicious looking plate.

"He said you should eat well to keep your strength since he had exhausted your favors."

"Oh, really? And just how was the master when you saw him this morning?"

"Not well." A slight smile tugged at Jayna's lips. "He looked to be a man with favors more exhausted than yours."

So, Rand had a rough night after leaving her to sleep alone. She had to wonder just how bad those nightmares were.

Or, maybe he just hadn't been able to sleep because he was missing her in his own lonely bed.

"Did he say when he would visit me again?"

"You are eager?"

"No! Not really. I mean, as far as masters go, he's probably not bad. I tried to bargain with him for those magazines and cards, so maybe that's what he sent with lunch. Yum. Looks good."

A bell sounded in the distance. Jayna cocked her head, nodded.

"It is permitted to bring the sheet in now." As Jayna moved toward the balcony, she paused. Her eyes were sympathetic and...

curious? "I hope it was not too painful, that the master was not unkind."

"He wasn't."

With a satisfied nod, Jayna opened the balcony doors and retrieved the hanging sheet, followed by boos of protest from below. A moment later Jayna was back inside, balcony doors sealed shut behind her, while she gaped at the sheet and shook her head.

"I hope he is a kind master, but I would not guess it from this!"

Rachel gasped. No wonder the depraved crowd had been cheering. It had just been a small vial that Rand had told her to pour, but she had dropped it in her urgency to get her hands all over him, then proceeded to wallow all over the sheet that looked like Andy Warhol had gone to town with a tube of Marilyn Monroe's lipstick.

"It wasn't as bad as it looks," she assured Jayna. "Really, it wasn't." She did *not* want Jayna thinking the worst of Rand. Not only because he didn't deserve it, at some point they would need Jayna's loyalty to them both.

"Here, let's just fold that up and put it away." Rachel thought of how Rand had wanted them to handle the sheet together, almost like a ritual, and she knew what it signified. It was theirs now and she did not want Jayna or anyone else to have knowledge of that intimacy. She left the bed, fully naked, and extended her hand. "I'll take the sheet now, Jayna."

Brown eyes that had seen a lot narrowed, scrutinizing her. Rachel didn't blink. She wanted hers and Rand's sheet back in her possession.

"You do not appear the worse for wear," Jayna decided, slowly handing the sheet over.

Rachel forced herself not to grip the sheet to her and kiss it, to bury her nose in it and smell him, what they smelled like together. Instead she quickly folded the ceremonial sheet, shoved it under the bed, and said, "The master may want that for a souvenir—

maybe enough that he'll trade me some more favors for it. Gotta use what leverage I can, right, Jayna?"

"Indeed, Mistress."

"Rachel, remember? When the master's not around."

"Of course. Rachel." Jayna suddenly busied herself with the cart and when she spoke there was an interesting inflection in her tone. "The master asked that I make you ready for his continued pleasure. And he asked that I tell him when you are ready."

"Anything else?"

"He hoped you would like the present he sent. That it would keep you company when he is not here to preoccupy you instead. I hope it is a good present since you may not emerge from the palace for six more days."

"What!"

Jayna shrugged, gave her "that" look. "It could be longer should the master choose. But according to custom the love slave is not allowed in public until he has had her all to himself for a full week."

"A full week!"

"Yes," Jayna informed her, which Rand clearly, and conveniently, had not. "Perhaps you wish to see what gift he has given you to enjoy when he is not enjoying your favors."

Rachel forgot about the delicious looking lunch that she suddenly had no appetite for. Friday was five days away, just do the math.

She grabbed the long pretty box with a white bow on top...

Wait. He'd wrapped his present up with the white silk that had bound her wrists at the auction.

"There'd better be some cards in here," she grumbled, carefully fingering the bow. "Magazines, too." Hopefully he hadn't thrown in a couple of tampons and a box of condoms to get his jollies at her expense. He could have such a sick sense of humor. "If he didn't then I'll take everything back about him being not such a bad master, all things considered."

Under Jayna's watchful eye, Rachel tore off the silk, tore into the box...and blinked. Somewhere in the center of her chest every mean thought she'd had about his latest lack of divulgence dissolved.

"Perhaps he is truly kind," was Jayna's observation. "I have never seen a master give such a gift as this."

No cards. No magazines. No inside joke with some tampons or condoms thrown in for shits and giggles.

Rachel gently lifted the doll that was dressed in a local costume and was ever so perfect...except that one of her button eyes were missing.

That sonofabitch. That impossible, wonderful sonofabitch, he never missed a trick. He was giving her the closest thing she had to home and winking at her while he did it.

There was an envelope at the bottom of the box that Rachel was itching to tear into. But she had to get rid of Jayna first.

"I have no idea what the master was thinking to give me something like this—she's even missing an eye! Sorry that he didn't come through with those cards he said I could have if I didn't scream too loud when he had his way with me."

"Perhaps the master's way is to say something that he does not find easy to say?"

Rachel met Jayna's curious, yet wizened gaze, and ad-libbed with an "I know nothing" shrug.

"Guess I'll find out. He's got me trapped here for six more days and after that, who knows? Maybe he'll go get himself another bed slave at the next auction and forget about me."

"I do not think so." Jayna pointed to the beautifully plated lunch. "You should eat, Rachel. And be glad that your master is so generous. It does not happen often, but the masters are not always so bad, and the women they buy come to have true feelings for their masters. I think you might have some already for this man who has been said to have paid more for a woman to warm his bed than any other in all of the auctions before."

"And just how many auctions would that be?"

"I was bought at one of the first." Jayna seemed to be doing some kind of mental figuring. "I was sixteen. I am now sixty-two."

"Do you have any children, Jayna?" Why she asked Rachel wasn't sure, it just seemed the right question to pose while she tried to thicken their sisterhood that Sarah was depending on.

"I have been barren despite many opportunities to conceive." Jayna looked up. "Sometimes the heavens are kind...but sometimes not, it would seem."

Jayna's heavenward gaze turned directly, frankly, on Rachel.

"While you eat to keep up your strength, I will draw your bath. Perhaps your next favors will win you cards and magazines to enjoy when the master is not around to entertain himself with you."

It happened so fast that Rachel couldn't say for sure, but she thought Jayna gave her a conspiratorial grin before leaving her behind with a one-eyed doll and an envelope that had a single word centered in bold script that read:

TWEED

The message inside said:

All I have to do is put my nose to your neck and I'm lost, no idea where I would be without you. I'm not sure if you want that emotional responsibility since I sure as hell wouldn't want it myself.

I saw a movie last year called Forrest Gump. I can't tell you much about the movie except for something Forrest said: "I'm not a smart man but I know what love is." I'm a pretty smart guy. But for a very long time, as long as I can remember, I have wondered what love is.

Note to self: Ever since meeting Rachel Tinsdale, you've been wondering if even a smart man might still learn.

Note to Ms. Tinsdale: Every charm tells a story; start with the house.

He had signed off with *Rand* but a swath of white-out had concealed his original signature.

Rachel scratched. She scratched some more, trying not to destroy the most meaningful message she had ever received. And then she whispered the letters:

"J-o-s-h-u-a."

Joshua?

What? Was Rand Slick an alias? Or, maybe Joshua was his middle name...but if Rand was one of those people who liked to go by their middle name because they got stuck with something like Herbie for a first one, then he would have introduced himself that way. And he wouldn't be covering it up with white-out, like he had changed his mind about the disclosure, but hadn't changed it enough to throw the note away and do a rewrite.

Rachel fingered the uncovered clue.

Rand had told her he was a man with closely guarded secrets, a past she didn't want to dig up. Apparently Rand Slick had a previous identity to conceal. Given his position in the high stakes world of finance, she could only imagine how truly lonely it had to be when a single slip to the wrong person could risk exposure on a very public stage. The question was, just what did he have to hide?

She turned her attention to the charm bracelet that had reminded her of a Monopoly board lined with silver trinkets. Players pieces. She had puzzled over them because they all seemed random, except for maybe the Queen of Hearts, and she liked to think that was a nod to her.

Rachel unclasped the bracelet from her wrist, laid it out beside his note. From left to right she took stock:

A little house

A doll

A shoe

A train

Timepiece dangling in the center

Racecar

Queen of Hearts

Tiny globe on an axis

A thimble

Armed with his new clue, "Start with the house," Rachel worked in sequence.

Okay, they were in the "house" Rand had told her they would be sharing together upon their first meeting.

Check.

Doll? She had a new one on her bed to remind her of the Raggedy Ann she had practically loved to pieces that was in her bookcase in Vegas. Rand had given her the bracelet after the night she agreed to take his case so maybe that was a sly reminder of just what had happened on her couch with Raggedy Ann and Daddy in the flask observing from her bookcase.

Check. Check.

Now, the shoe. It wasn't exactly like the fine wing tips he always wore, the kind that had first walked through her office door with some really nice cashmere socks. No, this was a runner's shoe, more like an old pair of Keds.

Hmm.

As for the train, more hmm.

Rachel moved on to the dangling timepiece that kept real time and was waterproof. Coming from Tiffany's, she was pretty sure it wasn't a Timex.

She considered the racecar, Queen of Hearts, the real little globe on an axis. Maybe that much made sense—their time in the car that set the wheels into motion, she was the Queen of Hearts in Sin City, only for them both to be spun into a very different place on the globe where next...a thimble showed up.

The man was a rhyme wrapped in a riddle and the more he entrusted her with the less she seemed to know. What she did know was that she wanted every little scrap of all that he had carefully hidden to everyone—everyone but her.

"Mistress? Rachel? Your bath is ready. It is not too hot. Not too cold. Just right."

Rachel instinctively placed her palm over the bracelet, the note.

"Jayna, you sound like Goldilocks."

"Who?"

"Nevermind. I'll tell you later. Maybe while we play with those cards I'm going to get one way or the other."

"I have never played cards but they must be much to your liking. You are so determined."

"Jayna," Rachel assured her, and she wasn't thinking cards, "You have no idea."

As Rachel made her way into the sunken pool of a bathtub, she thought about the charms, their sequence, about the events that had led her here...about what events could have led Rand to assume an alias...

Oh. *Oh.*

She wasn't looking at the time line right. That had to be it. He was Joshua before he was Rand and whatever events had led him to change his name could start with the house.

"You are sure that despite the sheet, he was kind?" Jayna gently asked, taking her off guard.

"He *is* kind," Rachel asserted.

Too late she realized how forthcoming she had been, judging from Jayna's raised eyebrow, her widening of eyes.

"At least, I think he is," Rachel quickly amended. "Guess I'll find out for sure once we have a spat, and you can bet we'll have one if Mr. Master thinks he can tell me what to do and I'll just do it to please him. Yeah, that'll happen. Like, when pigs fly."

"But pigs do not fly."

"Exactly."

Jayna laughed the way Rachel imagined her laughing before she had been bought on an auction block as a young girl, before life had become a hard teacher and she had been handled far less kindly than she had been herself.

Removing her headdress and tossing it aside with a little smile, Jayna casually observed, "You are not wearing his bracelet."

His bracelet. She had only told Jayna that a special someone had given it to her. Careful. She had to be careful until they had a solid baseline of trust. As much as she wanted to come clean, and she wasn't thinking the loofa with scented oil Jayna was putting to her back, it was too soon to fully take Jayna into her confidence. According to custom she was stranded inside for a full week before it was okay to venture outside—*thanks Rand/Joshua for failing to mention the first Friday at the bathhouse is a no-go*—so she and Jayna had plenty of time to feel each other out, judge how safe they really were with each other.

"It was a gift from my old boyfriend," Rachel hedged. "Back in America, before I got kidnapped and brought over here."

"This old boyfriend must be missing you. Maybe even looking for you?"

"I'd be real disappointed if he wasn't and still isn't." Honest enough since she hoped that Rand was missing her, and would come looking for her soon, even if he was under the same roof.

Rand plowed a hand through his hair as he paced his private office in local attire. He had so much experience playing various roles it shouldn't be so hard to slip into this newest disguise that didn't entail a bespoke suit, initials on his cuffs, Brioni ties, and shoes that presidents wore.

And let him not forget the socks.

Each and every detail of his outward appearance was as exacting as a movie set. The script edited to perfection. He just hadn't counted on a woman so saucy and sweet, so wise and yet so innocent, to completely disrupt his carefully constructed façade that could crumble in an instant with a single misplaced divulgence.

She knew his real first name now. Rachel would have noticed the white-out, would have been compelled to uncover what he had not completely disguised.

He had given her a tidbit, and like breadcrumbs leading to the witch's house, she was on the dark trail that would ultimately lead to the truth of who and what he really was.

If he had learned one thing in life it was that everyone was made up of who they wanted to be, who others thought they were, and there was a lot of obfuscation on both ends. Everyone's life story, at least to a degree, was a mixture of fact and fiction—his being more fiction than fact.

Rachel was the only one privy to more of the truth than not, albeit with limited information.

Rand considered the insider trading information on his Eames desk.

He hadn't gotten this far by playing clean. Arbitrage was his nice part of the business, and it wasn't so nice. He did junk bonds and other shadier aspects of finance that a Big Swinging Dick leveraged their compromised ethics on. Michael Milken had been his idol until his idol ended up in jail, thanks to the SEC.

He knew the SEC was now watching him. As well they should.

For so long his singular goal had been to amass an indecent amount of money, initially for Sarah, only for Sarah to become more like elevator music in the background while he shot to the top and wished there wasn't so much gum sticking to the shoes that kept him running in a place he couldn't escape, no matter how much money he made.

And now here he was: Having this witchy woman with raven hair and ruby lips prepared for his Devil's bed. And there was no question that she held him spellbound, moon in her eye, if he was seriously considering the merits of sacrificing many millions of dollars by not acting on the insider info he had never been reluctant to exploit before.

Rand made the call to a major source of his income and didn't give a rat's ass if it was 3 a.m. in the morning on the other end.

He laid down the phone, softly. His hands were steady but he could feel his heart race.

Him and Rachel. They were doing it for real on Zebedique time. Tonight.

CHAPTER 14

"You look lovely." Rand gave a polite bow at the Master's Chambers door but didn't immediately go for a kiss or even a touch to her cheek before he began to prowl the large space they were supposed to share but she had spent most of the day in solo, being "prepared." The routine was the same with the makeup and pampering, but she'd picked the gown this time and went for a nearly see-thru number that had her assistants laughing when she said they'd just see who the real master was around there.

"Thanks, Mr. Master," Rachel said, disappointed that he wasn't roaming his hands all over her already, what with all the candles she'd lit and the Tweed she'd put to her neck so he could be lost without her some more. "Me and all my assistants did our best."

Something was off. She could feel it in his silence, the way he picked up the doll he had given her earlier—then quickly returned to the bed as if ridding his hands of something he'd rather not touch.

"I did something today," he said abruptly. "I did it because of you, and I'm not sure how I feel about it."

"Sounds serious. What did you do?"

"If I told you then I'd have to tell you more than you already know. And I'm feeling like you discussing your menses, a little too much exposed."

Rachel wasn't quite sure how to deal with this side of Rand that was closer to his pen tossing Kong, albeit on the chamber pacing DL, than the Loverboy she had been expecting.

"Want to talk about it?"

He turned and his windows were more closed than she'd ever seen them before. Shit. What was going on with him?

"You'd like that, wouldn't you?"

"What?"

"You'd like me to tell you everything. Satisfy your curiosity."

Rachel started to retort, "My curiosity?" with some indignation. But that would be a lie when she had never been more curious about anyone else in her whole entire life. And she had known some real characters.

"Yes," she honestly told him. "I would like that. To know everything about you."

Rachel made sure the chamber door was solidly shut and strode to the pin cushioned bed where she had earlier rehearsed some unexpected moves of her own: Body draped seductively; back supine on the mattress. Lips moistened. She gave the doll a little kiss, tossed it aside. A crook of her finger, ruby polished, and she beckoned him to join her.

"God, how do you do it?" she heard him mutter while he turned an almost anguished expression upon her. "Rachel, you're killing me."

"Then why don't you come here and let me finish off the job?"

As if that was all the invitation he needed Rand unbuttoned his tunic, bared his chest, dropped the cloth to the floor.

"The rest?" Rachel gestured to his tenting trousers.

"I would prefer that you take them off for me."

"Of course. All in a night's work for a concubine."

Instead of coming closer he paused, placed a terse command: "Open your legs first."

"No." Rachel crossed them. "Not until you open your arms and come to me."

Rand wasn't sure how to react. He felt so vulnerable and exposed that he'd just tried to level the playing field with a crude demand—only for Rachel to make a demand of her own and pull him as inexorably closer as the tides to the moon while systematically knocking the supports out from under him—*boom, boom, boom*—with the accuracy of a velvet wrecking ball.

"I'm not who anyone thinks I am." He took a step closer to the bed.

"So I gathered…" She splayed her arms wide. "Joshua."

"You don't know what you're asking for."

Now she spread her thighs.

"Quite the contrary, I'm pretty damn sure that I do."

Up until now he'd at least felt like he was in charge of parceling out how much he told her, how far and how fast they went. And just like that, Rachel had seized the control he clung to and pushed him over the edge with the cunning instincts of Cleopatra summoning Marc Antony to her bed.

He stripped off the remainder of his clothes, came naked to the bed she was presenting herself upon with her barely contained breasts, her thighs parted like butterfly wings, just begging to be unwrapped from the nearly see-thru gown she had greeted him in.

"I hope you know what you've asked for," he said roughly, not trying to disguise what she had unleashed. "Because, baby, now you've got him."

Down his mouth went on her throat while he ripped aside the next to nothing gown and thought about turning her over, leaving the imprint of his palm on her sweet little tush until she begged him to ride her into the proverbial sunset.

But that would just be some payback for her taunting and bending him to her will—and, she'd probably like it.

This wasn't about liking. It wasn't about the payback he felt perfectly entitled to dish out.

This was about whether or not she could accept the unvarnished version of a man who didn't come with initials he had made up on the cuffs of the best shirt money could buy.

"Now," he said next to her ear, "I'm going to give you what you want, but we'll do it my way. I want you to feel at least a little of what I'm feeling."

"And what is that?"

Was she really ready for this? he wondered and fingered what she had offered. Oh yeah, she was ready. This girl liked the darkness, she liked the danger. Good thing since that's what she was getting.

"Invaded." Her gasp coincided with his careful but insistent upthrust while he continued, "Here's the thing about invasion. It's not necessarily unpleasant—in fact, I've found much of your own invasion into nearly every aspect of my life to be so pleasant as to be addictive. However, you've asked for access to areas that I'm not comfortable with at all myself. It makes me feel like it's too crowded inside, almost like I can't move without banging into walls that are closing in around me." God but her walls were sweet, melting all around his tactile invasion and melting him in places a Big Swinging Dick hadn't known existed. "How are you doing so far...a little too much yet?"

"No, no," she assured him. "Please. Go on."

Her palms roamed over his chest, moved lower. Rand gripped both wrists with his free hand, cinched them above her head and held them as they had been at the auction, minus a rope and a hook. The look he gave her was severe, cautionary, or as much as he could manage while her kohl-lined eyes, cast in candlelight, searched his and melted him some more.

He really did NOT want to be melting right now.

"I don't want you to touch me. Not yet. And I don't want you to talk. Your voice invades me as much as everything else about you and I can't have that messing with me at the moment. Nod if you understand."

Even the way she nodded, with her hair strewn over the pillow and smelling fresh as sweet morning dew, made a mockery of his resolve to show her exactly what she was getting if she wanted to crawl into bed with the "real" Rand Slick.

Resting his head on the pillow they shared, he closed his eyes, and like a bad Brothers Grimm fable he began, "Sarah was five and I was twelve when my father died, none of our piss poor relations wanted us, and the system decided to split us up...."

And as he told Rachel about leaving Sarah, jumping the train, the bum, even the five dollar bill and landing in Chicago, he was there all over again and yet he wasn't because he had a thumb working her cleft and two, then three fingers providing a physical touchstone between warm, tight walls alternately expanding and contracting, her internal flesh weeping as it accepted his rhythmic, in-and-out invasion.

"Oh my God," she panted, "Oh my God. And what happened next?"

"Shhh," he reminded her. "No talking. Especially not now, because this is where things get ugly and your voice, it's so pure to me that it just makes everything I'm about to say feel even more tainted. I'll spare us both the worst details, but when I couldn't make a living shining shoes and someone who looked like a system worker approached me, I learned how to convincingly lie, how to steal, and run really fast. I did what was necessary to survive where addicts and the underbelly of society live, if you could call it that. My education wasn't bad, considering I spent as much time as I could at libraries because there was heat that didn't come out of a barrel when it was freezing and cool air when my clothes were drenched in sweat and I couldn't afford a laundromat. I love libraries. It's where I started to envision a different version of myself, one I could make up like a character in a novel if I acquired the right manners, right clothes, got in with a certain level of society that had something I needed…and, as it turned out, needed something from me." He took a deep breath, steeled himself. "Something that's legal in Vegas. It helped that I was physically blessed in more ways than one."

Rachel's hips stilled. But she didn't dry up. At least not yet.

He lifted his head from the relative safety of the pillow and looked her full in the face. She was flushed but her eyes were wide open, unblinking. Knowing.

He let go of her wrists. She touched the jaw he had instinctively clenched. "It's okay. You can tell me."

"I was sixteen when I moved out of my hovel and into a nice apartment provided to me by my first 'benefactor.' A beautiful woman, wealthy, twenty years older, neglected at home. She was the first of several. I was also approached by men, some of them married to women who didn't know they were serving as beards, and all of them having more to lose than me if I didn't keep their advances—politely rebuffed—to myself. I was tempted to pad my pockets with some blackmail, but never went there. Call it my shining hour. Some of them are actually providing the current means of Zebedique contacts and helped orchestrate my atten-dance at the auction."

"So you blackmailed these past, ah…*ahhh*…associates to help you out all these years later?"

"Obviously no one from that part of my past is particularly worried about me outing them now or sharing any of our dirty little secrets since I have as much, or more, to lose than they do. Mutual blackmail should never be underestimated as a great insti-gator for Détente."

She closed her eyes and he wondered if there would be consequences for any of this, if there would be some straining of their own relationship that would need easing.

"Heard enough?" he asked.

"Not nearly," she said back and instead of pushing him away, wrapped her arms full around him.

It was the all-encompassing embrace without contingencies he had been longing for...forever.

"My real name is Joshua Smith. No one knows that but Sarah, and now you. When I last saw her she was fourteen and I was twenty-one. There was a small window of time she was alone but I didn't approach her."

"Why not, Rand? Joshua? What do you prefer?"

"Rand for now. But considering the way this thing is going with us, that could change. We'll see." As he removed his hand from between her legs she made a sound of protest, then a sound of invitation when he straddled her hips. But that's as far as he would go until they got something very important straight. "I didn't approach Sarah because I knew what I had become, and that she was better off without me. You'd be better off without me, too, Rachel."

"Don't say that. It's not true."

"Yes, it is. I'm damaged. Unclean. I was a whore. And I'm still a whore, just to a different master called money. I've been dirty a very long time. You're the only thing that's made me feel clean in twenty years."

He made to get off of her and that's when she gave him exactly what he craved to hear.

"No, don't leave me!" Frantically she grabbed him back, gripped him to her, perfect pale legs a vise circling his thighs. "I need you. All of you."

"How much do you need me? Enough to beg?" He felt like a scarecrow smiling down at a predatory canary building a nest from the dry straw he'd been stuffed with. "What you have to understand, my dear, sweet girl, is that underneath, deep down, I'm corrupted—and that part of me is really pissed that you have the kind of hold over me that you do because I like it on top and want you on your knees."

"Maybe Mr. Slick does, but Joshua's not like that, is he?"

"I thought you wanted all of me."

"I do!"

"If that's really the case, you can't have one without the other. Mr. Slick can screw you until you can't walk then cut you off if he feels too cornered and honestly, after this little chat, I'm feeling a very real urge to fuck you and run. That's what I know. It's familiar and safe. But this other guy, this nice, decent kid who didn't get a chance to grow up normally, he wants to shower you with affection, with roses and bracelets, even a doll. Let me tell you, it's been terribly annoying. An angel on one shoulder, devil on the other, both whispering what they want to do to you and it's like stereo with Metallica jamming with Bread in my ears. And now that you know the real lay of the land, the internal hardscape vs landscape you might say, the decision as to how we proceed from here is yours."

He watched her taking his encoding apart, considering the actual generosity of what he had just offered her: If she wanted it nice and sweet, the best part of him, he could deliver. Sometimes. But if she really wanted all of him, it was a package deal and she could never say she hadn't known exactly what she was getting.

Rachel suddenly, urgently, thrust up her hips.

"Then fuck me." But just as she brought his mouth to hers she whispered, "And make love to me. I meant what I said. I want all of you."

Rand knew he might just be learning what love was, but even a dumber than dumb man didn't need further invitation.

He had carnal knowledge of women's bodies inside and out. He knew all of the mechanics, the hot buttons to hit, just the right things to say whether he meant them or not. But as he touched, explored, kissed his way down from sweet hungry lips to an arching neck that drove him even more out of his mind with her scent, then to breasts he could bury himself in and die a happy man...

He was in terra incognita.

For a moment he thought of turning her over, learning each notch and curve of her spine, but that meant he'd have to stop his laving of her belly and release his hold from the hips he gripped. The span of his hands formed a perfect fan from both sides to where his thumbs met at her navel, her skin so pale and soft against his that he could hardly tear himself away from the vision to continue working his way down.

And then he was there, between her shaking inner thighs, and he could hear the low moans only he had ever called up from her— yes, he knew she'd never made that music for another man. It was music more seductive than a Red Shoe Diaries soundtrack and every note belonged to him.

Fuck her and run? God. No. Not tonight. Maybe not ever.

He'd never been in love before so he wasn't completely sure, and he didn't want to profess anything that he wasn't completely sure of because that would be breaking the most precious promise anyone could make, and any promises made from his mouth to Rachel's ear, he would not break...

But. If she couldn't hear, he could practice saying what in his heart of hardest hearts he really wanted to say, couldn't he?

As his mouth took ownership of her most private of private parts that danced under his tongue, Rand tried to form the words that had become so foreign it was like trying to speak a new language.

"I...I love..." He took a deep breath and out rushed his murmured words into the wet heat of her haven: "I love you."

Her lower body responded as if hearing what her ears had not.

Hips arcing sharply, heels pounding the middle of his back, hands tearing at his hair, the voice he couldn't get enough of demanding, "Give me! Give me the rest. You. *You.* All of you. Please, Rand, *please.* I'm begging."

Lifting himself up so his entire body cloaked hers, he wasn't sure just who she was getting because Rand Slick had company. Joshua Smith was right in the sack with them, his virgin penis poised to enter a woman for the first time in his life on a silk pin cushioned bed in a despised foreign country that may as well have been the back of a Buick on a deserted Lovers Lane with Mellencamp singing a little ditty about Jack and Diane.

But unlike a horny kid in adolescent love with more hormones than experience, he forced himself to pause. "I don't want to hurt you. We'll take it slow, in increments." Just saying the words had him enlarging even more, if that was possible. He was at a point of actual physical pain from his withholding and watching her take the condom from his hands, watching her sheath him with it then lick the tip...

Oh, man. Forget physical pain. He was in agony. And she was saying, *"Now."*

For the life of him he couldn't refuse her, couldn't refuse everything inside of him that culminated in the absolute urgency to take the virginity she was offering while he reclaimed some rare part of his own.

She felt like a champagne bottle, make it Dom, with him, the expanded cork, intent on containing her nectar while she urged him on, drank him up, until he couldn't stop himself from a final, decisive plunge.

Amazingly she took him. All of him.

What happened between them next was outside any experience he'd ever had. His hands and mouth all over her, his body inside of hers, invading and yet held captive. It was rapacious. It was divine. The fluids from her tongue joined his until he sipped the tears sliding from her eyes while her inner walls wept and damn near milked him dry.

He wasn't particularly sweet, but dear God she was; and then he was, and she wasn't. It reminded him of when he once watched two finches in a birdcage, a male and female, the way they alternated chirps and made a completely unique song between them.

Theirs was a song made up of whispers and harsh breathing, of moans and hungry growls. They should have both been hoarse by the time the sun pinked the sky when, in the midst of their languorous aftermath, she cupped his head against her chest. Rand could feel the soft up and down movement of her breathing, and cosseted between her breasts, her hands gently stroking his hair, he was aware of an unfamiliar and yet distantly familiar sensation —like he was truly cared for and protected the way he hadn't been since...

Since he'd inhaled the same smell. Before Sarah was born.

Rand felt like he'd just been zapped with a thousand volts of buried electricity erupting from the middle of his chest and radiating into his loins, and not in a good way.

He leaped off the bed, leaving Rachel with thighs spread and him with a condom filled with what he'd wanted deposited straight into her, drooping like a sad balloon from between his own thighs.

"I know that smell. I've known it since we first met and the smell of you drove me wild. My mother wore it." He clenched both hands into his already rumpled hair. "You smell like my mother and all I want to do is crawl all over you, I don't care where. Does that make me a pervert?"

For a moment Rachel gawked at him. Her mouth and eyes three huge O's, like a cartoon character.

And then she started to laugh.

"A pervert?" she repeated. "Are you kidding? It just means your mom had great taste in perfume."

Her glistening thighs opening wider, Rachel murmured, "Now come back home to Mama." An enticing twist of her hips and she added with the blow of a kiss, "Baby."

They alternately made love and fucked like mad for three nights and days straight. Rachel told herself it was okay since she couldn't leave to do her job for the prescribed period that didn't involve her period at the bathhouse anyway and they had another four days left to indulge their insatiable appetite for each other before she could even venture outside without breaking protocol, which wouldn't be a smart thing to do.

God bless the completely screwed up laws of Zebedique.

He fed her lamb, smoked lox, cheese and grapes while they hydrated with more wine than water before they fucked and made love some more.

The only thing that bothered her was that Rand always disappeared in the wee hours, before returning mid-morning, bearing more food.

By Saturday—one week exactly since he'd bought her at the auction—and after way more trips to the bidet than the toilet, just as Jayna had predicted, Rachel decided she'd had enough. Well, at least for a few hours.

"What? You're tired of me?" the Lone Ranger asked, while she felt like a well broken in "Hi-Yo, Silver, away!!"

"Never that," she truthfully answered him. "But Rand, I'm worn out. And besides, if I don't better befriend Jayna, we may never get out of here. Tomorrow's a big day."

"What if I said I don't care? What if I said…"

"Yes?" She knew what she wanted him to say.

He didn't. Instead he popped a grape into his mouth, got out of bed, and aggressively put on his barely worn clothes, his eyes never leaving hers.

"Fine. I understand. We're here for a reason. I'm being selfish. It's a not so healthy part of my nature. Sorry. But not really. Of course you need some time alone, even if I don't for a change. I'll have some cards and magazines delivered ASAP so you and Jayna can hang out and make progress. We'll have dinner together tonight and pick this back up for dessert."

"Rand," she said tenderly, reaching for him, wanting him back already.

"I treasure you, Angel." He kissed her forehead while firmly extricating her arms from around his neck. "Later."

And with that Rand Slick, aka Joshua Smith, was gone.

CHAPTER 15

Sunday arrived with Rand absent from bed of course when she awoke, but it was nonetheless an important day in terms of what was about to go down outside of the Master's Chambers. They were going to walk to the market and would casually pass Sarah's house of incarceration on the way back with Rand's men following them, and Jayna acting as guard over his newly humbled bed slave.

Rachel was pleased with the progress she felt she'd made while teaching Jayna how to shuffle a deck and the basics of Rummy. She'd easily won the first hand but was surprised when Jayna beat her at the second. Good for Jayna, even if, like Rand, Rachel didn't like losing.

"Sorry we didn't get to the magazines yesterday," Rachel told her while Jayna adjusted the veil covering the face she wasn't supposed to show to anyone but Rand, unless you counted the peekaboo eye-slit, making her feel more like Casper than some indecently priced bed goods.

"There will be time," Jayna assured her, only to grin and say, "Besides, I would rather play cards."

"You're a natural, Jayna. Next up is Poker. Just set you loose in Vegas and you'll be buying Liberace's estate."

"Liberace?"

"Great piano player into candelabras and swinging onto the stage with wires." Rachel thought of what Rand had told her, about being propositioned by other men he had turned down but had somehow continued to curry their favor minus blackmail, or most possibly the lack of it. Rand did have friends. They just weren't the usual, and when you got down to it, the usual was pretty boring. "I saw Liberace once. I was just a kid but he was really amazing."

"I wish I could see this Liberace," Jayna said wistfully.

"Sorry, he's dead now. But there are lots of other acts I'd love to take you to if we could just get the hell out of here and head straight for Vegas."

Jayna nodded, then as if catching herself, sternly shook her head. "It is good to dream, but not to dream for too much."

"No it's not," Rachel muttered then seized the moment to firmly assert, "No. It's not. My boyfriend could be looking for me, Jayna. He's smart. He's connected." She jangled the charm bracelet on her wrist. "If he finds me and gets me out of here, I could take you with me. You'd be free. How would you like that?"

The hope that immediately brimmed from Jayna's eyes just as quickly evaporated.

"I have friends, a family here. Leaving them would be hard, but what you describe is impossible. Be kind to yourself and put your dreams away so they do not torture you when they cannot come true. To even imagine such things comes with a heavy price. I know since I dreamed them once myself many years ago."

Jayna lifted her long skirt to expose her inner thighs.

They were scarred with what looked to be old knife slashes and burns. Rachel swallowed back the bile rising in her throat and remained silent.

"What you see are signs of shame that I endured after I tried to escape a master who was not so kind as yours. This was not all that was done to me, Rachel. A man may be made a eunuch, but a woman may be cut too." Her mouth trembled then grew hard. "I have no pleasurable woman parts left. They were cut out for my disobedience after I tried running away."

"Oh God, *no.*" Rachel choked, nearly gagging on the sickness in her throat. Her vision blurred and she grabbed Jayna to her. "I hurt for you." She could hardly get the words out, her horror and compassion were so complete. "How could that bastard do such a thing to you?"

"Because it was within his masterly rights." Jayna patted her back, oddly the one offering consolation. "And what your master, no matter how kind he might seem to be, will have the right to do also. Please. You must not cry for me. My next life will be better. And yours can be good now." She held Rachel away, gripping her by the shoulders. "I tell you this so you will be warned. But if you should ever be foolish as I was, I will turn my back when I should be guarding." She gave her a small shake. "Tell no one of this talk."

The desire to tell her all was great, but Rachel knew better. Jayna had suffered enough without being drug into this too—at least not until she could offer Jayna safe harbor. And she was getting it before they ever ventured into the bathhouse. Rand could figure out the details, call in whatever favors he hadn't called on already and blackmail whoever the hell he wanted if it meant getting Jayna out of this sick country with them.

The bedroom door opened without a knock of forewarning. Jayna quickly stepped away as Rand entered, looking as powerful and demanding as his role dictated he appear.

"Leave us, Jayna. I wish a few words with my bed slave."

Jayna bowed out, catching Rachel's eye then touching a finger to her lips in warning.

As soon as the door shut, Rand's stern mouth gentled into a

smile. If she hadn't been so upset she would have been struck by his almost boyish charm.

"Hi, Angel." He quirked a brow. "How did you sleep last night? No better than me, I hope."

"Rand, we have to talk."

He frowned. "What's wrong?"

He opened his arms and she sank into them, grateful for his solidity and strength and yes, moral substance.

"We *have* to get Sarah away from here."

"Of course we do." He lifted her veil and brushed a soft kiss to her lips. "After the market we're walking past her house so you can get a feel for the general territory. It's a good excuse to time the distance. Not that I'm sorry for the time we've had alone since you got here, even if it was extended beyond your initial expectations."

She gripped his tunic in both her hands. "It's not just that. We *can't* fail. If we do, what could happen to Sarah would be worse than if we'd never come at all. This country is vile. Slavery isn't even half of it."

"Explain."

She did, feeling his grip tighten with each appalling word. His expression revealed shock, grinding anger, and something she should have anticipated by now, but somehow hadn't.

"Forget the shopping and get packed. I'm calling for my plane. You're out of here in the next hour."

"What?"

"You heard me."

"But Sarah—"

"Sarah means the world to me, Rachel. But having one woman I love at stake is bad enough and I'm not going for double or nothing. Now get packed while I contact the men I've had watching her house. We'll just have to come up with a plan to abduct her. You're leaving."

Rachel knew a momentary dizziness, one part of her mind

sifting through what he'd said about not going double or nothing with the women he loved while grappling with the realization he was sending her away. What if he failed? What if Sarah's owner caught them? This was far riskier than their original plan. Sarah could be mutilated while Rand rotted away in this stinking country's jail.

"You can't do this, Rand."

"Watch me. It's my decision to make and it stands."

"But we both know how heavily guarded she is, why your men can't make a successful snatch. It's why you hired me. I can get to her where they can't. Don't do this, Rand. Don't do it to Sarah." She yanked the collar at his throat and brought his eyes even with hers. "Don't do it to me."

She saw concern slowly replaced by an implacable hardness, a calculating expression. Rand Slick in full business mode.

"Why? I'll still pay you in full."

"Really? You have the audacity to say that to me? You are so full of bullshit right now it makes me want to slap you silly. Don't be an asshole. We stick to the plan. We stick together. You're not sending me away. We all leave together—Jayna included—or we don't leave at all."

"Sounds like you've got it all worked out, Ms. Tinsdale."

"That's right, Mr. Master. I'm not going anywhere today but shopping with you."

Rand sighed heavily, shook his head. "I'm only trying to protect you. I'd never forgive myself if any harm ever came to you."

"The only thing that could hurt me now is if you send me away. Let me stay and do my job. We're partners, remember? I can't go back without you because I..."

She caught herself. Were her eyes giving her away, she wondered frantically, while his windows narrowed, probed, ascertained.

"Because...why, Angel? I'm waiting."

Rachel considered the wisdom, or folly, of speaking her heart in a way she had thus far kept silent. She knew she loved him. She was so deeply in love with him that simply looking into his eyes gave her the sensation of staggering, deliriously sliding headlong into a revolving glass door that was going too fast to escape out the other side.

The Master's Chambers had become their intimate womb. Once they were spit out on the other side of the world where this beautiful, erotic fantasy of theirs had to confront reality, there could be hard, emotional consequences if she let herself believe that what they had now would remain unchanged. Rand had made no promises. She would want them. She already did. But what good would a promise here be if he woke up in New York, safe and sound with Sarah, and wondered what the hell had he been thinking?

"Because I made a commitment, Rand. I made it to you, and commitments are sacred to me. Like promises are to you. So I guess you could say we're alike that way."

"No offense, but I think we're alike in a lot of ways."

"No offense taken."

His response was a raised eyebrow, as if he were waiting for more. She couldn't stand the taut silence, the churning inside her head and in her stomach while she felt a surge of empathy with Rand's ingrained need to run.

Rachel spun away, ready to dart for the door.

Rand grabbed her arm and jerked her back so fast her breasts collided with the width of his chest, pushing a soft "Ooof," of air from her lungs.

"Where do you think you're going?" he demanded, whipping the covering from her head and thrusting what seemed an uncommon number of fingers against her scalp, twisting round and about so that she had no choice but to stay put.

"I'm going shopping," she gasped.

"I don't think so. Not until we finish this discussion."

"There's nothing left to discuss. I'm staying. We're getting Sarah. You're going to get Jayna asylum, no matter what you have to do to make it happen. And now, Mr. Slick, you will let me go and we'll proceed with the day as planned."

"We're not on your couch," he informed her, eyes slanting, probing hers with the accuracy of a well-placed finger to her privates, only this time to the workings of her mind. "Now, if against my better judgement I agree to let you stay, there's something I want from you in return."

"What?" she asked warily.

"You've given and given to me without asking for anything in exchange. It feels a little one-sided and that doesn't sit well with me. You want more. I know you do. So, what is it? What do you want from me that I haven't given you?"

What do I want from you? I want you to say that you love me. That you can't imagine your life without me, no matter where in the world we are. I want you to say that you won't take it back once you don't need me in the capacity you hired me for, and that you want me to be the mother of your babies. I want you on bended knee. I want you to put a ring on my finger that I'll never take off, even if it's out of a Cracker Jacks box. I don't want you to just buy the cow, but the whole damn farm.

It was a bit much to ask. It was what she wanted him to freely offer, once this sting was over and reality had moved back in, separating them by 2500 miles with no rescue of a sister to keep them together. And so, Rachel compromised with what she truly wanted before reality slapped them both in the face.

"You're right. I do want more. I want you to sleep with me. All night. No staying awake until I'm asleep and you go to wherever you go to have your nightmares in another bed without me."

The breath he took was so sharp, the distress in his eyes so immediate, that her real thoughts might have possibly been a relief if she'd said them instead.

Now she really wanted him to stay the whole night.

"You drive a hard bargain."

"Like you said, we're alike in a lot of ways. No offense."

Rand let her go. He paced around, keeping his back turned to her as he considered whatever he was considering before whirling around, the dark windows of his eyes calculating.

"Let's negotiate. I'll do it. But not tonight."

"When?"

More dark window calculating.

"Thursday. The night before you go to the bathhouse and try to make the connection. If all the dominoes line up and we're out of here with Sarah—"

"And Jayna. We don't leave without Jayna."

"She's a complication we don't need."

"Everyone has plenty of complications they don't need. That's life, Rand. Step up to the plate, you'll figure it out. And once we're back on home turf, you can figure out some more about where your real priorities are in life." She squared her shoulders, put her Casper headdress back on. "I already know where mine are. I'll agree to Thursday for your overnight stay—if you'll agree to let me watch you shave. Ready to go shopping?"

She knew he was a man who thrived on being in control, and even with her concession of a delayed overnight stay, he clearly wasn't happy about the terms she had brokered as he reluctantly accepted with a curt, "So be it. You win. This time. Now let's get the hell out of here and go buy some souvenirs."

CHAPTER 16

*W*alking ten paces behind Rand, Rachel played her role of a just bought bed slave getting a public lesson in submission. Even so, she was grateful for this taste of limited freedom —and that Rand had listened when she warned him one chance glimpse of his sister could set off some dangerously instinctive reactions. He agreed that under no circumstances would he stop as they passed Sarah's residence and they would save their walk for dusk, when the shadows masked their faces and the hired surveillance tailing them at a discreet distance wouldn't be as easily noticed.

That had been her reasoning, though in truth it was a gut feeling she couldn't justify that something could go wrong. The feeling was still there but Rachel shook it off, determined to enjoy this bit of sightseeing while she could. Bathhouse Friday would come soon enough. She still had plenty of groundwork to lay before then, but today—her second, and hopefully last, Sunday in Zebedique—she'd savor.

The late afternoon sun slanted into the huge canvas tent as they filed down one row and then another, Rand the leader, she the chattel, and Jayna bringing up the rear as her guard. Jayna had kindly, but sternly, laid out the rules:

Slaves were not permitted to speak to their masters unless spoken to first. Slaves were not to make eye contact with any man but their master. Slaves were to keep the expected distance at all times, unless signaled to trot to his side should he want a fondle, then fall back the required ten paces once he was ready to move on.

To break any of these rules was to risk a public whipping.

Trinkets and fabrics and hand-carved wood, all vied for Rachel's attention. She paused to admire an ivory necklace. Jayna gave her a gentle push.

"Hurry, hurry," she urged. "The master walks on."

"But I want to know how much this—" A high-pitched wail stopped short her protest. Rachel searched for the source.

Close to where Rand stood, a good twenty paces ahead, was a spectacle that caused her stomach to lurch as it had upon seeing Jayna's disfigurement. A fruit vendor grappled with a dirty urchin-like child who dropped a banana as the man shook him.

Acting on impulse, she began to run toward the child. Jayna grabbed her arm and spun her around.

"Do not be foolish, Mistress. Else you suffer a beating."

"But that man, he can't abuse the poor child! Somebody has to do something!"

Jayna's grip tightened as Rachel struggled to intervene.

"You can do nothing. It is sad, but common to catch hungry thieves. The child will be punished. I do not wish for you to be punished also."

"Punish a starving child for stealing a banana? That's inhumane. What's his punishment, a spanking?"

"His hand will be cut off. It is the price all thieves must pay."

Such was her shock that Rachel stared dumbly at Jayna and

then at the weeping boy who begged for mercy. *What could she do?* She had to do something, anything, to stop this atrocity.

Rachel broke free of Jayna's hold and rushed forward. When she was just shy of the fruit cart, Rand confronted the merchant. She was close enough to hear his halting speech in the Zebedique tongue which the other man replied to with a rabid snarl and another shake of the wailing child.

Just as she was ready to join the fracas, Rand held out a thick stack of local currency and gestured to the fallen banana. The merchant hesitated. Rand withdrew the bribe.

Before Rachel could yell at him to give the man however much money he wanted, the child was dumped on the hay-strewn floor and a bunch of bananas thrust into his grimy little hands by the vendor—who quickly held his own palm up.

Rand shelled out the pay-off. The child kissed his feet and, hugging the fruit to his skinny bare chest, darted from sight. His savior appeared to take no notice, but Rand had turned his gaze on her and she saw the distress, the rage and compassion she herself felt, mirrored in his eyes. She stood only a few feet away, far closer than she was allowed.

"Woman!" he bellowed, and raised his hand as if he meant to strike her. "Will you never learn your place? Get back where you belong. Ten lashings await you at home."

He was so convincing that she instinctively fell back two paces and collided with Jayna. Several passersby shouted their hearty approval, no one needing an interpreter to know she'd just been royally admonished by a most masterful master.

She caught his quick wink as he turned and studied the vast array of exotic fruit. The rat. The stinking, marvelous rat. She loved him so much in that moment her throat constricted and her mouth trembled beneath the veil while she watched him select an assortment of cherries and figs, dark grapes and ripe persimmons. When he offered the vendor a handful of coins the other man refused payment and tumbled the fruit into a thin cotton sack.

Rachel assumed it was Rand's generosity in exchange for the child's hand that got him the freebies. Wrong, she soon realized. The man pointed at her and laughed, apparently impressed with Rand's hold over his concubine.

Rand slapped the man's back as if they shared similar philosophies on the debasement of women. She knew better. Though he smiled a tight smile, Rand's jaw was clenched and so was his fist around the sack. He looked mighty close to shoving the vendor's face into the wagon of fruit.

Rachel stepped forward in warning. Jayna clamped a firm hand on her shoulder.

"Do you wish for twenty lashes, Mistress, not ten?"

"For heaven's sake Jayna, he wouldn't—" Rachel bit her tongue. Like an amateur she'd almost slipped and come to Rand's defense. Amateurs and women PIs in love with their clients were not mutually exclusive. "What I mean is, the master seeks his own pleasure. He'd rather make me pay up in bed than beat me to a pulp."

"Yes. I think this too," Jayna agreed with a sly look. It was that of a wise older woman who'd endured enough pain to recognize love no matter its form or disguises. "Do not make him shame you again when it is not his wish. Be still now, for he comes."

Next thing she knew, Rachel was staring up at Rand's madder-than-hell face. He gripped her wrist and shoved the sack into her hand. If not for the soothing rub of his thumb to her pulse point or the apology she read in his eyes, even she might have bought his act.

"Carry this," he snapped. "You will feed it to me later." He matched his harsh command with a yank of the clasp at Rachel's temple.

His kiss was immediate, greedy and rough. It was a long kiss, so long she wondered if he meant to make out until dusk set in. Not that anyone around here took notice of such matters, judging from the activity that bustled around them.

Staying as true to her role as possible, Rachel refrained from gripping him to her, this man, her lover, her friend, her only link to Western civilization. Their kiss was confirmation of the bond they shared in this horrible place, where the people weren't right, not right at all. But in their midst was rightness— she and Rand, reassuring each other in a too strange land with his hands kneading her buttocks and her own clenching the bag between them to keep herself from returning his show of possession.

His mouth was still open as it skimmed her cheek and settled beside her ear.

"I hate this perverted country," he said so quietly that even Jayna couldn't hear. "I'm close to hating myself for being the one who got you into this. But, Rachel, I'm...I'm selfish enough to be glad you didn't let me send you away."

"I'm selfish, too," she whispered. "Even here I want to be with you. Especially here." The uneasy feeling she'd had earlier notched up despite the security of his nearness, and for good measure Rachel sternly reminded him, "Don't forget that if we see Sarah or her owner when we pass their house that you *have* to keep going. Don't stop. Don't even look their way."

"Understood. In the meantime, I think it's a good idea if you pretend I'm that jerk by the fruit stand who's watching us. Misbehave and give me a reason to play your master. Who knows? Maybe he'll toss me a pineapple or two."

"Yes, Mr. Master." Rachel reluctantly thrust him away. She wiped the back of her hand against her wet mouth and refastened the facial covering.

Rand's sardonic laughter echoed through the tent.

"Just a taste of what's to come, wench! Wipe your mouth again and I'll slap it."

He turned on his sandaled heel and didn't glance back. She waited until Jayna gave her a nudge...

And laughed softly behind her.

As they approached Sarah's street, the niggle of apprehension she'd felt earlier came closer to an alarming unease with each step toward their destination. Rachel told herself she was being ridiculous, that nothing could go wrong by simply passing the place Sarah was kept.

She shifted the assortment of packages in her arms while keeping her gaze locked on the back of Rand's head. An elegant black limousine whizzed past and turned into a driveway two houses down. Mansions they were, putting she and Jayna a good half block away. Rand sped up.

She could have been the perfect concubine instead of a palm-sweating PI the way she immediately matched his accelerated pace over the red brick sidewalk.

Her heart kept time with her feet, beating faster, faster. The swish-swish sound loud in her ears, Jayna panting as she rushed to pick up a fallen package.

"You carry too much, Mistress. Let me help."

"Thanks, Jayna," Rachel muttered distractedly. She thrust the bulk of her load into Jayna's arms, hardly aware that the elder woman struggled to grasp it all while she herself now carried nothing but a bag of fruit.

For a split-second, Rachel chanced a backward glance. The hired men, dressed in Zebedique garb, were making tracks behind them. They appeared to be deep in conversation but she was certain from their quickened march that they were aware of the sudden switch in what had been an innocuous walk home.

"Dammit," she groaned, cursing herself for taking her gaze off Rand for even that little bit. He was closing in too fast, but thank heaven not fast enough to beat the wrought iron gates that swung shut behind the limo.

She ran to catch up when he stopped in front of the gates. He stood there frozen, unmoving, as the driver got out and opened the passenger door.

What in the world did Rand think he was doing, calling attention to himself like that? It was exactly what she had feared. He didn't know what he was doing, wasn't capable of thinking past the instinctive need to reach his sister.

By the time she'd regained her ten-pace distance a man and two women had emerged. Rand still hadn't moved.

"You bastard!" Rachel dug into the sack and hurled a soft persimmon hard as she could. *Smack!* The juicy, melon colored orb splattered against his upper arm. Rand whirled around. "You sonofabitch, who do you think you are expecting me to bow to you?"

Fruit began to fly. A handful of cherries hit his chest, zapping her target like buckshot from a gun. Next, she launched an attack of grapes from his face to his crotch, screaming insults at his genital endowment as she advanced. By now the car's occupants had turned to observe what appeared to be a mutinous slave turning her owner into a living work of abstract art.

Several figs landed between Rand's stunned eyes before she pounced and knocked him on his butt. Rachel punched at his chest and kicked at his shins. She wrestled in earnest until he had no choice but to flip her on her back, sprawl his body over hers and lock her in a stranglehold unless he wanted the crap beat out of him.

Once his face was within inches of hers, she wheezed out in a whisper, "Get a grip, Rand. Get it and fast or you'll blow the scam. Hurry up and apologize to our audience for your wayward slave and let's get the hell out of here!"

He shook his head as if to clear it. Rachel pushed him off and sprang to her feet. There had to be a God in heaven because Rand followed suit along with her orders.

He thrust her away with ample momentum to send her stumbling backwards into Jayna and the two hired men who'd caught up.

While Rand made a stilted apology to the small gathering on the other side of the gates, Rachel insinuated herself between Jayna and the hired guns, hoping against hope they passed for locals enjoying a cheap thrill.

"Scram," she hissed at the two men.

They took off, laughing as if they'd just gotten their jollies for the night.

These guys that Rand had brought in were really good. But not as good as Jayna, sizing her up with a withering glare before scouring her with a string of scalding epithets, then throwing down the market's bounty and shoving Rachel to her knees.

Jayna's hands pressed against her charge's shoulder blades then moved to urge Rachel's face to the ground until her forehead rested by Rand's foot in humble, beggarly fashion.

Once the onlookers retreated to the house, Rachel felt Jayna's soft pat of reassurance and then Rand's tight grip as he pulled her to her feet.

The trek home was made with Rand, ten slow, deliberate paces ahead as if he struggled against nature to forge each step. Jayna, just behind her, sing-songing a litany that might have been a lullaby or a prayer.

And she, Rachel, thanking Jesus, God, Mary, and Buddha while she was at it, for their narrow escape while she cursed, yet understood, Rand's near fouling of their master plan. And while she thanked her heavenly benefactors, she thanked Jayna in silence. Jayna deserved better than what she'd been born to and Rachel was going to see that she got it—

Along with the screws put to this country and the slavers who benefitted from its twisted mass psyche.

CHAPTER 17

Upon their safe arrival back, Rand sent Jayna away, but instead of hauling Rachel up to the Master's Chambers, he said curtly, "Come with me," and took her to the realm where he felt most in control.

He shut his office door behind them, and even though nearly covered from head to toe in the evidence of her quick thinking and his complete lack thereof, he punished himself by leaving the hated garb on.

"Take off that ridiculous head covering," he told her, "Take it off so I can see your face and whatever disgust you must be feeling after you warned me, repeatedly, and I still screwed up."

She did as he bade her but all he saw was understanding in her gaze. "It wasn't your fault, Rand."

"The hell it wasn't! If you hadn't started pelting me with... with"—he gestured to the mess she had made of his clothes—"I was ready to start banging at the gates, crawl over them to get to her. It was Sarah. I know it was Sarah. And you saved her—and us—from no telling what because of me."

"Rand." Rachel came to him, where he had planted himself on

the edge of his Big Swinging Dick Eames desk—*Jesus H Christ, how could he have been such a stupid dick??*—and began unfastening his tunic.

Rand gripped her wrist. "Don't. You're cutting me way more slack than I deserve, but I won't have it. I'm so angry with myself right now that a fair sentence would be to rot in this thing and donate my suits to charity."

"But if you did that I couldn't get all excited thinking about taking those Gucci ties of yours off—"

"Brioni," he automatically corrected, anal-retentive, attention-to-every-detail control freak that he was. "Like that matters. *Ugh.* Just hang me with one right now."

Rachel tapped his terse lips with a gentle yet determined touch. Witchy woman, that's what she was, inducing him to take a little nip of a ruby painted fingertip. She tasted good. Like a mixture of fruit. Make it more like wine from the gods.

"You have to start forgiving yourself for being human. For making mistakes that anyone could make in the same situation."

"I don't want to forgive myself. I want to punish myself for everything I've done wrong, and there's enough of that to sink the Titanic. What in the world do you see in me, Rachel?"

"Apparently everything you don't see in yourself."

She moved away, giving him the space that he needed even as he felt the compulsion to plant her back against his desk, against the wall, on the floor. Didn't matter. He was absolutely consumed with the need to touch her, to fill himself up with her and pour all that was wrong with him straight into her willing body that...

Wanted all of him.

"Nice office," she observed, giving him a little smile before turning her attention to his bookcase. She began examining his books, as if she might learn more about him from the selection.

When she reached his favorite titles—*Barbarians At The Gate* and *Den Of Thieves*—she tiptoed her fingertips to *Liar's Poker* and pulled it out.

Bending slightly down, she took a look at what his very favorite book had covered.

"Well, what have we here?" Rachel worked the no longer hidden lock, opened the bookcase door to reveal his hidden sanctuary, and, "Voila! Hey, baby, you've been holding out on me. Cozy little place you've got tucked away in here. Mind if I explore?"

She didn't wait for his permission, just strode right in, and he wasn't waiting for her to stride back out while he tore off the tunic he wasn't going to rot in because it was going straight into the nearest burn barrel...or maybe he should keep it as a life lesson reminder. Along with the ceremonial sheet she had given to him and asked if he might want to bring it along as a "souvenir" when they made their escape.

Like she had to ask. No way was he leaving something so precious behind.

He followed her as she checked out his private study that would be at home at The Algonquin or The Bowery Hotel, storied New York establishments with many stories to tell. She gave a neat spin to the large Old World globe on an axis that parted in the middle. It was a mini-bar that housed his libations and if you opened the top up...

She did.

Rachel lifted the bottle of Macallan 20 Year Scotch he'd put enough bent into since their arrival to be reaching low tide.

"It helps me sleep."

"Want to finish it off?" She waved the bottle back and forth so the remaining amber liquid swished in invitation. "I'm not a Scotch drinker normally, but I could be if it's passed from your mouth to mine."

"I feel drunk every time you kiss me."

"Same here. Maybe we should go to Kissers Anonymous after

we polish off the bottle..." She moved further into his private quarters, from the study to adjoining bedroom. It was small. Nothing but the bed he thrashed upon at night and typically woke up in, feeling more exhausted than rested.

There was a large tiled shower adjacent to his sleeping space, where jets on the sides and rain heads above helped him wash away the remnants of night sweats. He knew he always smelled cleaner than clean, but no matter how many showers he took, he couldn't wash away the dirt and the grime that had clung to him since a bum had saved his life and hauled him into a railcar heading for Chicago.

Rachel hit the jets. Stripped off the subservient clothing that didn't belong on anyone but she made an absolute mockery of. She stepped into the stream of water coming from the top, the sides; shower massage in one hand, bottle of Macallan's in the other, she beckoned him to join her.

"So, what are you waiting for, big boy? C'mon, get naked with me. Let's drink. Let's get it on. And let's forget that it's been a really rough day."

She was, of course, returned to her pin cushioned Master's Chambers bed so Rand could sleep alone after they had polished off his Macallan's, tore up his sheets, and he'd apologized so many times about his screw up that she'd finally told him he should change careers and become a self-flagellating priest.

A light knock sounded at the door before Jayna entered, pushing the familiar food laden cart. Bouquet of roses on top.

Great, Rand. How discreet. Just throw another doll in without an eye missing.

Wink.

"The master sends his best wishes this morning," Jayna said

with a not-so-secretive smile. "Perhaps he has sent something else of meaning as well?"

Jayna got points for cutting to the chase. She raised the large domed lid of a tray to reveal the empty bottle of Macallan 20 Year Scotch beside a lovely omelet...with a button as garnish.

"Hungry, Jayna?" Rachel asked, deciding they were moving past Poker lessons and straight to the end game. "Happy to share."

"You have shared much already, but...yes. Let us share."

She handed Rachel a fork, which Rachel returned.

"You have the first bite."

"If you wish."

"I do."

Jayna forked up a nice piece of the omelet and savored the bite she thoughtfully chewed.

"You love him."

"No use in lying. I do."

"He is your boyfriend. The one who gave you the bracelet."

"He is."

"Why have you come here?"

"To save his sister. He's a good brother with a promise to keep and he hired me to help get her out of here."

Jayna extended the cutlery, raised a brow.

"You need me?"

"Yes. But Jayna, please know that as much as we need you, I haven't been working you as a means to an end—okay, cards on the table, that's not quite true. I thought you were a little scary when we first met and I knew we needed to be on good terms to meet the end goal, but since then, as Mr. Master—Rand—said to me once, a lot has changed. We have to get his sister, Sarah, out of here, and us along with her. We need your help. And in exchange, we'll get you out of here, too."

Rand was still working on that, but he could make it happen. He was a rainmaker in finance. He could make rain wherever he chose with his contacts in high places if he was willing to trade favors.

Rachel didn't give a damn about what the exchanges might be, she just knew that however dirty he had to get, the outcome would be clean.

"What do you need me to do?" Jayna asked, fingering the button garnish, then pushing it to Rachel's side of the plate.

Rachel returned the fork in exchange. "I need you to find out who's guarding Rand's sister and if she could be a potential ally. We'll get amnesty for her too if she's in." So, she'd stretched the truth. But once they got on the plane, good luck to the good old U.S. of A to explain their reasoning for re-depositing innocents back to a country that could consign them to a fate worse than death for simply speaking a horrible truth that needed international exposure.

Rachel believed in the country she'd been fortunate to be born in. She had more appreciation than ever for the freedoms she'd once taken for granted. Never again.

"I have family here," Jayna explained. "I would have to leave them to possibly suffer the consequences of my own freedom. They could be punished."

That added a whole new layer of complexity to an already complex situation.

Rachel combed her brain for a solution. The one she came up with wasn't perfect, but it might work.

"What if you appeared to be abducted by us, against your will? What if you wrote something, like a letter, saying how awful the American master is and you're afraid of what he might do? Leave it with your relatives for proof. Then once we have you safe, we could work on getting them away from Zebedique, too."

Jayna shook her head. "I know what you see and you only see the bad. But there is good here, too. Wherever families are, even in hard places, they have their sense of belonging to what is familiar.

And to each other. I do not think they would want to leave..."
Jayna took a really big bite of the omelet before pronouncing,
"Even if I do."

"Then you might help us?"

Jayna, clearly the sharpest crayon in the box, ascertained, "His
sister, she was why he stopped at the gates, yes? Her guard is
Montage. Montage is my friend. She has no family left and still
holds the dreams I once had of escaping."

Yes!! "Jayna, would she know of Sarah's cycle—if she will be
allowed in the bathhouse this Friday?"

"She should know. I will ask."

"And you're sure that Montage wouldn't say anything to Sarah's
master?"

"In private she spits after she speaks his name. He is not a kind
man. The sister has not been treated well."

Rachel considered the wisdom of sharing that with Rand. As
instinctively protective as he'd been the day before, he didn't need
more fuel to ramp up his rescue ambitions.

"We won't tell the master—Rand—about that." Rachel imagined
herself slipping and calling him "Master" once they were back in
the States...presuming there would be enough opportunities to
slip.

"I am afraid I ate most of your breakfast," Jayna apologized,
offering the fork for a final bite.

"No, you go ahead and finish it, Jayna. I just thought of something that kind of made me lose my appetite."

"Do you wish to talk about it?"

Rachel shook the head she had to keep in this game. "No, but
could you draw me a diagram of the bathhouse layout?"

"Yes, I know the bathhouse well. And many of those who work
there."

The sketch Jayna provided was incredibly valuable and so was
her insider information. She offered to bring Montage to meet her.

"I'd really like that opportunity, Jayna, but I'm afraid of raising any suspicions with a personal visit. Will you act as our go-between and do all the communicating for us?"

"Of course. What do you wish me to tell her?"

"For starters, not to breathe a word about this to Sarah."

As he studied Jayna's sketch in his office, dressed in a suit he'd decided he wasn't ready to donate to charity, Rand could not believe how much Rachel had accomplished, even learning that Sarah would be at the bathhouse on Friday. He wasn't exactly happy about their escape party of three expanding to five, or bringing not one, but now two refugees, with them, but so be it.

"I told her that Montage needed to keep this on the QT from Sarah."

"Good idea. There's no telling how she might react. For all Sarah knows, I'm dead."

"How are you feeling about seeing her again?"

"Anxious. Nervous. Thrilled. Of course she might harbor some deep seated resentments against me. As she should. A lot of years have passed since she looked at me like..." Rand shook his head at the memory of when. "Like I'd hung the moon and could swing her on a star."

Witchy woman leaned over his desk, knuckled his jaw. "Of course you could. I should know since you've taken me to the moon and back."

Deserting his executive's chair, he came around to crook a finger under her chin, tilt it up, to better search her eyes.

"We need to talk about what's going to happen after Friday."

"No." Raven hair bounced with the adamant shake of her head, only for ruby lips to assert, "No. We have too many unknowns waiting for us there and when I think about it...it upsets me. I can't afford to be upset, Rand. I have to be absolutely focused on the here and now. We'll just have to figure things out as we go."

"I understand. But I want some assurances. I want to know

you're not going to dump me, decide I was telling you the truth all along, that you'd be better off without me."

"Trust me, Mr. Slick, the doctor here has more at risk once her patient is cured of his missing person affliction."

"You haven't slept with me yet."

"Care to bump it up by a few days?"

Now it was his turn to do some adamant head shaking. Just thinking about it made him feel queasy. He had no idea what might happen if his little demons decided to come out and play as he shared a pillow with his sweet little witch. Yes, somewhere along the line, Little Miss Red had turned into quite the sorceress.

"Okay, we'll stick to Thursday. But meanwhile, maybe you'll indulge me and let me watch you shave?" She lightly ran a nail down the prickle of his five o'clock shadow. "C'mon, baby. Be my Gillette man?"

And just like that she had him smiling. Oh yeah, she'd cast one helluva spell on him.

"Sure. Is now soon enough?"

"No, a month ago was. But as they say, good things come to those who wait."

He couldn't wait to oblige, just so he could bury his freshly shaven face between her breasts, between her thighs, slide it up from the small of her back to the nape of her neck, and not abrade any of that softer than soft skin.

"After you," he said once Rachel had done her "Voila!" thing again with *Liar's Poker* plucked from the bookshelf.

Maybe he needed to expand his reading choices.

It was the first time she had divested him of his tie, then the shirt with initials on the cuffs that had begun to feel more like a branding iron than a statement of Big Swinging Dick couture.

And as he leaned into the mirror, watching her watch him shave, Rand decided it was time.

"I love you, Rachel." A swipe of blade over chin. "I've been practicing saying that. I haven't said it to anyone since I left Sarah, and I wanted the moment to be right when I told you what I've never told another woman before." In the mirror he could see her eyes light up, shimmer. "I didn't want to tell you in the heat of a moment, though I have many times now, you just couldn't hear."

"Why...?" She put her hand to her throat. "Why now?"

"Because it's not in the heat of a moment and you can never doubt my real sentiments are sincere. And unless I'm terribly mistaken, I think there's a good chance that you love me too." Razor pause; his eyes engaged hers, a reflection of somber brown meeting luminous green. "If you aren't ready to say it back, a nod will do."

"I...I..." She blinked. She nodded. Several times in quick succession. "Of course I love you. How could I not?"

"Maybe because I have such a hard time loving myself." He put down the razor. Turned. No more mirror exchanges giving them a minor distance. He brought her hand to his freshly shaven cheek and pressed his lips into her palm.

"Rand," she whispered.

"Call me Joshua. I want to know how it feels to hear you call me by my given name."

And she said, "Joshua."

It felt odd to hear her call him that, call him by a name no one had spoken since...she had beckoned him to bed and parted her thighs while she gave up her virginity and restored some of his in the process.

"Not a bad name. I'm okay with it. At least with you. I've been Rand longer than I was ever Joshua, so it could take some time to get used to." Time. It was not on their side to seal the most important deal he'd ever brokered. They had three days left before everything changed. And it would. She knew it. He knew it. He had to secure something...something between them that would bridge all that they had thus forged into an uncertain future.

He could ask Rachel to marry him. But that wouldn't be fair. He'd never had previous difficulty in being unfair, but he couldn't do that to her. He was her first lover. He longed to be her only, couldn't bear the thought of her sleeping with another man. But Rachel had to be the one to make that decision once she had the freedom of choice, which she hadn't had here. And, too, while he had an exorbitantly successful career, hers was just getting off the ground and could really take off upon their return. He had no right to cheat her of what he had enjoyed himself and she had more than earned.

Rachel feared he might leave her for what he was returning to once they left Zebedique? How naive.

"So," he finally said, still unsure of what the something was he could use as binding collateral. "Assuming that everything goes according to plan on Friday, and that's assuming a lot, we land back into the States with Sarah, Jayna, and now Montage. As for where that leaves us—you and me..." The taste he took from the delicious lips she was worrying beneath his considering tongue gave him a much needed sense of security. "I love you. You love me. We have that verbally established now and I don't believe either of us will renege on such precious words. Trust is a rare commodity in my life, but I do trust that no matter what happens, we have what it takes to see our way through. And now that we have that squared away, I have just one more question to ask you."

"Yes?"

While strains of Carole King broke up the battle of the bands between Metallica and Bread, Rand came as close as he'd ever come to a proposal. "Will you still watch me shave tomorrow?"

CHAPTER 18

*T*hursday arrived. Rachel wondered if she had a single nerve end that wasn't quivering in anticipation of "Bathhouse Friday," which had become code between her, Jayna, and Montage for their master plan of escape. According to Jayna, Montage was full on ready to go. Jayna had a small bag packed of her most important keepsakes and a letter to declare her innocence in the possession of her family. Rand had all the other details addressed: Backup muscle. Car on ready for getaway. Two guns—both for her since he'd never shot one. Plane waiting on the tarmac.

Neither of them said anything as they mostly just looked at each other across the bowling alley table and barely touched a delicious last meal of braised lamb, fragrant minted couscous, and an assortment of culinary accompaniments that were completely wasted on them both.

As she continued to gaze at Rand in his fine black linen tunic and he continued to gaze back at her in the gown he had selected for their first night in this very room, she wondered if he too was remembering when she had asked him if guys ever got butterflies in their tummies, of what had followed with the blood, the ceremonial sheet, the "everything but" before she fell asleep in his arms —and woke up in bed alone.

She knew Rand was dreading the night and wondered if he would simply try to remain awake, when the last thing either of them needed was for him to be sleep deprived in their most critical hours of escape.

Maybe she should let him off the hook. But…no. Rand wasn't the only self-serving person at the table. It was odd how they had started to assimilate certain qualities of the other. He seemed a little more like her in ways, and she, him. Is that what happened to married people?

For the umpteenth time she thought of that fleeting moment when her heart had pounded like mad from her chest to her ears while she thought he might propose, only for him to ask, "Will you still watch me shave tomorrow?"

Rand suddenly pushed back his chair that resembled a throne and rose majestically from the table.

"Woman. You will leave your chair now and come to your master."

The sound of his command conveyed a different message than it had that first night. There was no playfulness in his tone or expression. And she didn't pretend outrage or strut like a burlesque queen his way.

Head tilted back to look deeply into somber brown and completely open windows, she asked quietly, "Yes, Master?"

"I'm not hungry," he confessed.

"I am." She wrapped an arm around his neck, pulled him closer, and into his ear she breathed, "For you."

This time he didn't haul her over his shoulder. This time she didn't pretend to struggle and wail an indignant protest.

He offered his arm and with a sense of decorum, escorted her up the grand marbled staircase they would not be ascending again. Once they descended, they were leaving and would not be coming back. Rand already had everything he considered of value packed and put on the plane.

Candles illuminated their Master's Chambers cocoon. Beside their silk pin cushioned bed was a tray where two crystal flutes were waiting, champagne on ice.

"I can't believe I'm saying this," she whispered, "But I'm going to be sorry to leave."

"Yes," he agreed. "I feel the same, Angel."

He hadn't called her that for a while.

"We feel a lot of the same things, Rand." She placed his hand over her heart. "Make love to me?"

Slowly he removed the gown he had removed once before. His touch was different now; no longer exploratory, he touched her like he knew her body better than she knew it herself. And the way she unbuttoned his tunic, stroked her fingertips over his chest, was the touch of a woman who could live to be 100 and never forget the beauty of this man in his prime, the feel of him under her hands.

Their coupling was tender and yet there was an underlying desperation she sensed between them, and Rachel knew what it was. They were saying goodbye to what had become familiar and were trying to hold onto its last traces as long as they could.

Much to her surprise, Rand actually fell asleep before she did. She studied him as she'd never been able to before, his head heavy on her chest. Light snore. She stroked his hair with one hand. Tipped champagne to her mouth with the other. He seemed so peaceful, why had he been so worried about sleeping together for the first time?

Then he muttered something, gave a little jerk. Another one followed. The glass in her hand shook—

Only to fly skyward with his violent flail, a sudden shout of, "NO! Get away from me! Not that hungry!"

"Rand." Rachel slightly nudged him, kissed his forehead. "Rand, wake up. You're having a bad dream. Wake up. I'm here."

His eyes opened, startled, terrified. But he didn't seem to see her, only the remnants of whatever ghouls induced him to protect himself with an upward sweep of his arm.

Her head rocked back as his defensive maneuver connected with her cheek.

Rachel had no idea what to do. She had tried to imagine what his nightmares might be like, but she hadn't imagined anything like this.

There was no rationale to her reasoning. She simply acted on instinct and climbed atop him. She planted her lips on his and sucked up his nocturnal whimpers. And as she did, there was a whisper that came from some primal part of her core, one that said, *You know what you want this last night. Take it. Take what he's never offered and right now, like this, he won't refuse.*

He wasn't completely erect, but that didn't stop her from sheathing what she could, feeling him as intimately as possible, no condom to intrude. Her menses was due in a few. They should be safe. *But what if it's not?*

Rachel ignored this other voice, the one that prided itself on good morals and ethics and reason.

He quickly began to grow, bloom inside her, reminding her of a sapling shooting up and out to become a full grown tree...or like a boy growing into a man.

She rocked into him while he laid there, quiet now. Rachel couldn't tell what his state of consciousness was, shutters closed over dark windows. If only she could crawl through them, maybe she could see the remnants of his bad dream, and if she could she would chase down his bullies and shoot each one deader than dead, so none were left that could harm him.

"Come," she whispered. "Come to me."

Down she plunged so he was buried inside her from root to straining tip, and she threw back her head as she ground into him until she felt her uterine contractions.

It was an incredibly intense orgasm but she made not a sound. Not even when she felt his own body's responding release and the sequence of hot spurts that set her off again.

His eyes were still closed when she looked again. His breathing had quickened, but there was no indicator as to whether he was awake or had ejaculated in his sleep.

Rachel knew she should feel guilty. She had made an executive decision without Rand's agreement.

Maybe she had more of Rand in her than a flaccid penis that she reluctantly gave up. After all, she didn't feel guilty in the least.

As Rachel drifted off to sleep to join him in slumber, she knew she'd do it all over again given the chance. Because they were leaving tomorrow and no matter what happened thereafter, no one could take from her what she had extracted from Rand in her greatest time of need.

And should there be any consequences for her actions? The tradeoff for this was worth it and she would hold no one accountable but herself if the piper wanted his pay.

Rand waited until he felt Rachel slightly drool on his chest. She was a mouth breather in sleep. He had watched her sleep many times, but as he slanted his eyes to the top of her head, he saw her a little differently.

He knew what she had done. And he had allowed it. They were two complicit thieves stealing what they needed from each other. While he wasn't sure what Rachel's need or motivation was exactly, he certainly knew his own: It was the something to secure their future he had wanted while his higher nature called on him to be fair. There was no collateral more binding than two people in love making a child. If by some miracle he had gotten Rachel pregnant then she would have to marry him—it was that simple. He wasn't about to have any child of his grow up without a father, and that would totally justify his withdrawal of fairness to Rachel's decision making about her future love life and career.

Stroking his fingers through her hair, he wondered how much she had witnessed while he grappled with his demons in what had been a very deep sleep. Apparently what she saw hadn't scared her off since his familiar re-visitation of being chased by a gang then beaten bloody for stealing a bag of Fritos from one of them had faded, only to culminate in the realization that his dream girl was on top for a change and putting him inside her...no condom? No condom.

He had pretended sleep. Let her take him however she desired. It was a very different kind of taking than his previous arrangements with perfectly nice, wealthy, attractive women who liked to fawn over him while he thought of them more as his over-indulgent and somewhat sad clientele.

He owed most of them far more than what he had given in return. They were, collectively, largely responsible for his ultimate success. Between their discreet introductions to professional contacts in the higher echelons they circulated in, monetary gifts and tutoring in the social graces, and his consumption of every money magazine, business book, and Wall Street Journal he could get his hands on, he had his ground floor footing. And then, with the instincts of a shark, the cunning of a snake, and hunger of a pack of starving wolves, he had removed himself from their company and started calling his own shots.

Maybe he would tell Rachel about all of that one day.

But for now he would secretly relish this last night in Zebedique with the witchy woman that, more than anything, he wanted to make his wife.

He hoped Rachel had gotten herself pregnant. That would make his own future selfish decisions far easier going forward.

It was his last thought before he succumbed to a sweet, dreamless sleep.

Rand wasn't sure what awoke him, feeling more rested than he could remember in his adult life—and he had been an adult for a very, very long time.

Perhaps it was the trill of the first morning bird singing its song outside the balcony doors. Or, it could have been that he had slept through most of the night—not counting his little wake-up call post-nightmare—and had overreached his typical wink-eye quota.

But he was pretty sure it was because Rachel, legs hooked through his, arms draped over his chest, had stirred.

He had decided that he would play the innocent, "I know nutting" Schultz card. If Rachel wanted to come forward before the final results were in, that was up to her. If the results came in positive, however, all bets were off. He would haul her over his shoulder to the nearest Justice of the Peace if he had to. Vegas. Yeah, baby. They knew how to make what should be lifetime commitments happen quick.

She yawned, languorously stretched. She combed a hand through his chest hair and muttered, "What time is it?"

"Time for you to wake up and give me a good morning kiss." He put one to her forehead.

He didn't have to ask twice. She rose from his chest and planted a kiss straight on his lips while he planted one back. If either of them had morning breath, who knew and who cared.

It was only after Rachel broke away to catch a breath and shake out her fire breathing mane of curls that he noticed...

"Rachel." Unlike the moment he had recognized the original source of the cologne that drove him wild, he didn't spring from the bed. He touched her cheek, red and swollen, with fingertips that had begun to shake. "Rachel, look at me."

She did with limpid pools of green.

"What happened last night, while I was sleeping?"

Her look of sudden guilt told him that they weren't in the same wheelhouse of reasoning.

"You...you were having a bad dream. And I...I..."

"No, this isn't about you. It's about what I'm afraid I did to you." He traced the swollen area of feared contact and battled the immediate urge to vomit. "Did I hit you? Did I do this?"

She caught his hand. "It wasn't on purpose. You didn't do it deliberately."

"Oh God," he groaned. "Oh God."

Now he put her aside, got out of the bed. His nighty-night hopes that she might have gotten pregnant did a complete 180.

"Rand, please stop pacing around like some lion in a cage. Come back to bed."

"No," he said miserably. "No, I can't."

"Then at least look at me."

He made himself do it. He made himself look at the physical damage he was responsible for. And then he couldn't. Just couldn't. It was worse than any nightmare he'd ever endured.

He turned away, gave her his back.

Her arms came around his waist, hugged him tight. He felt the heat of her struck cheek rest between his shoulder blades.

The utter love and acceptance he felt in her embrace only made him feel worse. She was so pure compared to everything he was, and now he had the evidence to prove it. Never had he experienced such self-loathing, the desperate need to distance himself and run.

"I love you," she told him, followed by a soft kiss to one stiff vertebrae notch and then another. "Please turn around and look at me."

He tried. He really tried.

Rand shook his head, hanging so low his morning stubble abraded the chest she never should have slept upon.

"I can't look at you. If I do, I have to look at the worst crime I've ever committed, and I've committed enough to be doing some serious time. No, Rachel. I would do anything for you, and the best thing I can do now is to keep you safe with my distance."

Her sharp smack to his back brought his head up. Red talons sinking into his biceps caught him so off guard that he didn't have time to resist when she yanked him around to face her.

"Stop it," she snapped. Her eyes snapped too, an infuriated shade of green that refused his gut churning need to look away. "There's a difference in deliberately hurting someone whether you love them or not, and what happens when you're not capable of making that choice. You didn't hit me because you wanted to. You did it without intention. I have no doubt that you'll be beating yourself up forever for something I could never blame you for at all. But what happened, happened. And you know what? The timing couldn't be better."

Rand couldn't think past his abhorrence of her swollen cheek moving as she read him the riot act.

"What do you mean?"

"What I mean is that what we've got here are some lemons that have you feeling really sour about yourself, but now that we've got them, we shouldn't let them go to waste. I'm going to use them. Make lemonade. Appearing to be a little beat up will help me out at the bathhouse. I won't stick out so much if I look more like the rest of the girls who don't have a master that's quite as kind as mine."

"Kind?" he scoffed. "Oh, yeah. Kindness is me."

Rachel suddenly pushed him away with a snort of disgust. "Enough of your pity party, Mr. Slick. We have important business to see to. Time to dress and get this show on the road. We'll pick this conversation back up once we're out of here. Goodbye Zebedique. Hello, freedom—and to whatever happens once you have your sister back and we're living on opposite sides of the coast. We can figure our shit out once we're in our respective offices. Already feels like a Barnum and Bailey railcar full of elephant poop."

CHAPTER 19

*R*achel sat close to Rand in the backseat of the Mercedes limousine that would be their getaway wheels. She knew his distress was equally divided between the drum-roll of getting Sarah out of the bathhouse and into the car, and the fact that he'd hit her, even if unintentionally.

One look in the mirror and she'd gasped at the sight she made. Just a little higher and she would have looked like Spuds Mackenzie with a big black ring around her eye. As it was there would be a decent sized bruise on her cheek, where it was already puffing up like a marshmallow, only about the size of a large fist.

She covered the one he was clenching in his lap. Rand didn't move his hand away but he didn't offer to open it and hold hers, either.

Bastard. He should be holding her hand right now, giving her all the encouragement he could. But, no. He'd rather wallow in his own misery than put her first.

"Hold my hand." It wasn't a request.

Rand hesitated, then complied.

Jayna watched from the other side of the seat that faced them. Eyes narrowed; lips pursed.

Rachel could still hear their earlier touch-and-go conversation when Jayna came to help her dress.

"Mistress! What has happened? Did the master do this terrible thing to you?"

"It was an accident, Jayna. Rand wouldn't—"

"But he did, did he not?" Jayna spat on the floor. "I do not know if I can help him now. He does not deserve to have his sister back if he is no better than the master she has."

"No, no! It's not like that. Rand is a good, good man. He has night-mares and tried to warn me but I insisted and when he started thrashing I got in the way of his arm. He's horrified about it and feels a million times worse than my cheek does. Please, Jayna. Please. You can't back out now. Two wrongs don't make a right, and nothing could be more wrong than not getting Sarah away—and you away, too."

"And Montage."

With that concession Rachel knew she had things back on track, but it had spiked her anxiety, which she really didn't need after the whole fiasco with Rand. Jayna didn't trust men in general, and rightfully so, but unfortunately Rand was now the recipient of her scrutiny.

The car rolled to a stop. The driver, one of their hired men, parked a discreet distance from the bathhouse entrance.

A quick glance out the back window assured Rachel their backup had parked two lengths behind them.

Rand checked his watch. Gave them a tight, forced smile that was more a grimace of encouragement.

Jayna adjusted her headdress.

Rachel did the same and double checked that the two guns were exactly where they should be, stashed inside a leather satchel under the seat: a Glock 19 with 15 rounds already loaded, and a

Beretta automatic 92C with enough magazines to take out a small army.

"Ready, Jayna?"

"Yes, Mistress."

"Then let's rock and roll. It's Bathhouse Friday. Showtime."

Driver in costume got out. Opened their door. Jayna emerged first. Rachel gave Rand's hand a squeeze and let go, only to have him pull her back in when she had one foot on the sidewalk.

He pushed aside her headdress, kissed her fast and hard.

"I love you. Good luck."

As she walked away Rachel could feel him watching her retreat. Her pulse was racing but at least her hands felt steady, her mind clear. She didn't envy Rand having to stay put with nothing to do but watch slow-motion minutes tick by and try not to imagine what could go wrong as she and Jayna disappeared through a pair of shiny brass doors.

Soft lighting greeted them, a soothing contrast to the sun's brilliant rays outside. The entry itself was immense, and thankfully cool, giving way to columned arches, gold urns housing lush palms, and decadent rooms smelling of jasmine. Groans of pleasure from cushioned massage tables reached her ears, as did murmurs of conversations in various languages and the universal sound of laughter from the direction where she knew a huge bathing pool would be.

Rachel removed her headdress so anyone around would presume she was just another bed slave that had gotten slapped around by her master. Jayna scowled.

"You are sure that he—"

"Jayna, I'm sure. Trust me, any guy who tries to rough me up is missing his nuts in the morning—and the master's were definitely intact the last time I looked." A flash of crawling on top of him and grinding herself down to his base made her breath catch.

She would have to think about that, about what she had done and why...later.

Although Rachel knew the layout by heart, she let Jayna lead. They had their roles to play and their strategy down pat. It was simple strategy. Easy as 1-2-3:

1. Montage was to already be here with Sarah. She would be sure that Sarah was in the sauna.
2. Jayna would wait outside the sauna doors with Montage while Rachel went in and made contact, hoped Sarah kept her cool, and could follow the remaining orders.
3. They would get dressed. She and Jayna would leave first. Montage and Sarah were to follow behind them. They would get in the car, and then it was pedal to the metal to their waiting plane.

Jayna pointed her towards the dressing area where she efficiently got Rachel out of her clothes and into a Turkish towel. From there they took a leisurely walk through a voluminous chamber where naked female bodies in all sizes and ages appeared to be in a state of nirvana as they soaked in the massive communal tub. It bubbled like a vat of champagne, triggering another flash: champagne flute shaking then flying from her hand with a sudden outcry from Rand and—

"Stop it," she hissed.

"Did you say something, Mistress?"

"No, Jayna. All good." She estimated they had less than a minute before they reached the sauna where the most privacy was to be had. The timing was important so Sarah wouldn't get too hot and try to leave.

Just then Jayna was hailed by an old colleague, and then another, until there was a small group gathered round her. Jayna, apparently well-liked and missed by her bathhouse buddies, darted an anxious glance at Rachel.

If there was anything she hated it was rudeness, but Rachel didn't think twice about whining, "Jaaay-na, can we please go to the sauna?" She lightly rubbed the major league bruise that was forming on her cheek and winced. "My face hurts and that will make it feel better. Or, if you want to visit with your friends, I can go by myself, and when you catch up, maybe you could bring me some water?"

Jayna spoke quickly in the local dialect and amongst understanding nods and brief hugs the group surrounding them dispersed.

"What did you say?"

"I said that you were a pain in the buttocks and I would come visit with them later because the master would be angry if I let you out of my sight."

"Jayna? Once we're back in Vegas, maybe you'll want a job as my assistant. We make a good team."

It wasn't the grateful smile Jayna gave her, but the glistening in her eyes that laid a hand on Rachel's heart. These were Jayna's friends. She may never see them again. She was going to a foreign country to start over and not at a young age. Virtually everything and everyone she knew, she was about to leave behind.

Rachel simply nodded her silent understanding and on they went, each step forward a step closer to Sarah, a step closer to their ultimate escape.

They reached the area dedicated to several separate sauna rooms. Jayna went directly to the middle one where another guard was posted. Rachel could only presume it was Montage, who confirmed it when she whispered, "Bathhouse Friday," like she was really getting into spy code mode. Her eyes sparkled with barely contained excitement.

At Jayna's nod, Rachel entered the sauna, a nice sized room

billowing puffs of steam with carved benches against mosaic tiled walls.

The door closed and a quick survey informed her that two dark skinned women were enmeshed in a private conversation while another one, blonde and very pretty, slouched on a bench seat near the back. Her eyes were closed but Rachel discerned dark circles of fatigue beneath them. A purplish bruise rode high on her cheek.

As Rachel drew closer, the impact was immediate and forceful. She didn't need a recent photo to know this had to be Sarah. With such a strong facial resemblance to Rand there was no question they came from the same gene pool.

"Hey," Rachel greeted her quietly. "You look like you could be a fellow all American girl."

The woman raised up and looked her full in the face. She smiled tiredly, as though the spirit had been beaten out of her, then indicated Rachel should sit.

"Welcome to the club." She made a derisive sound. "Been to any good auctions lately?"

"Yeah. But I think we've got a little more in common than that and getting nabbed at a Vegas casino...Sarah."

Her deep brown eyes blinked several times. "How do you know my name?"

Rachel put a finger to her lips, nodded toward the other occupants.

"I'll tell you in a moment, but let's start with me telling you my name is Rachel Tinsdale. I'm a private investigator who was hired to get you out of here by someone who's been trying to find you for a very long time."

"Who...?"

"Joshua."

Sarah's mouth worked but no words emerged and Rachel patted her hand.

"It seems there's a promise your brother is here to keep. He's waiting in a parked car nearby. My job is to make sure you get in it."

"Joshua," Sarah whispered in a faraway voice. She choked on a muffled cry. "I can't believe it."

"Believe it." The two other women continued to talk and Rachel hurried on. "We have to move quickly. What I want you to do is count to one hundred after I leave then get up and follow me out. Everything's set, all you have to do is finish your sauna, get dressed, and walk."

"But my guard—"

"No worries. Montage is coming with us."

"Joshua." Sarah was crying. "Joshua."

"Sarah, I need you to stay calm, okay? We can't pull this off if you fall apart, so just try to blank out everything except my instructions. Come on, I'll start counting with you. One... two...three..."

"Four...five...six..." Sarah continued the numbers as she swiped at her cheeks.

"Good girl." Rachel squeezed her hand and got up. She nodded amiably to the two other occupants who sent her a cursory wave and continued their gossip. At the door, she stole a look at Sarah who gave her a tremulous smile and kept counting.

Ten minutes later, Rachel exited the bathhouse with Jayna, turned in the direction of their waiting car. They had only taken a few steps when she heard the anticipated swing of the bathhouse door, followed by the sound of footfalls behind them. A quick glance assured Rachel it was the company they had come for.

She recognized the nondescript car with their cover on ready to pull out as she heard the limousine's engine start and purr. The back door opened when she was less than five paces away.

It was then that she heard the sudden shout. A cry of outrage screaming obscenities, while the sound of running feet pounded too close behind them.

CHAPTER 20

*R*and's gaze was fixed on Sarah—*God, was it really her?*—when he heard the man's harsh shout.

"Stop!" His robe flapped while rolls of flab bounced up and down in time to his agitated jog. "Stop, stupid bitch! Where do you think you are going?"

It had to be Sarah's owner, a repulsive insect of a man, inducing Rand to surge from the car.

He grabbed Rachel and shoved her into the limo, pushed Jayna in behind her, while Sarah ran to him. Any thoughts he might have had for a warm reunion fled as he thrust her in the same direction and barked, "Get in!" Her headdress covering came loose, exposing a large, ugly bruise that he knew wasn't accidental.

The older woman who had been running with her stopped, whirled, and hurled herself at the greasy looking pursuer while she screamed, "Go! Go now! *Aghhh…*"

Rand rushed to her as Montage reeled back from the fist that caught her in the face. He disentangled her from the enraged piece of excrement that came at her again and needed to learn it wasn't nice to punch out old ladies—not to mention his sister.

"Get in the car. Get out of here and don't wait for me. I'll follow."

With that he jerked Sarah's owner by the robe at his throat and shook him as though he were a mouse caught in a cat's mouth. They were in the middle of the sidewalk and a car whizzed past without stopping, the seediness of the country allowing public brawls.

In spite of his girth, the bastard managed to twist free and land a blow to Rand's jaw. Amidst spitting curses and spittle in his face, Rand's street smarts took over.

Uppercut to the right, fist to the gut, and a knee in the groin that should have him indefinitely singing soprano should have been enough. But it wasn't. Rand wanted to kill him. He threw his punches like he was working out on a side of beef.

"You filthy sonofabitch." Another brutal jab. "That's for beating up on my sister. How do you like it, huh, huh?" He grabbed him by the hair and nodded his battered face up and down. "Feels real good, right? Big man like you, so tough you go hitting old ladies..."

He might have literally beat him to death, heaping murder on top of any other charges he might have to face, but for the sudden clench at his shoulders, pulling him off. He whirled around, ready to push the intruder aside. Rachel caught him by both arms.

"Rand! Rand!" She shook him hard. "Oh God, Rand, please stop. He's not worth it. We have to get out of here while we still can!"

He had trouble focusing he was so blinded by his vengeful purpose, but she was pulling at him, pleading with him, and then raising her own fist as if she might knock him out and drag him away herself. Rand was suddenly aware that a crowd had begun to gather, some placing quick bets and shouting "More! More!" while others called out for the police and a doctor.

He caught Rachel by the waist and they began to run. The split second they made it into the car, the driver peeled out before he could shut the door.

Rand was breathing raggedly, the fight still in his blood when he felt a shaking palm cover his hand.

"Joshua?"

Staring at his sister who sat by his side, the years rushed in reverse. All the rehearsed words of apology and reunion deserted his head and all he could say was, "I finally kept my promise, Angel."

Then Sarah's arms were around him, and his around her, clinging as close as the day they'd said good-bye.

"I always knew you'd come back for me," she said brokenly.

Rand used the edge of his sleeve to dry her tears and wipe her nose. He wished it was one of his dress shirts instead of the Zebedique tunic he couldn't wait to put to a Bic.

"I have something for you."

He reached across the seat and discovered Rachel held his gift in her hands. They connected, hands touching, gazes meeting in a silent understanding. *Bless you,* was the message his eyes sent. *Bless you for giving me Sarah back.* Rachel's chin quivered and out rolled two big tears. His throat tightened, knowing she was shedding the tears he couldn't because big boys didn't cry.

Placing his offering in his sister's lap, he said, "I thought you might want to hold your doll on our way home."

"Home," she repeated, stroking the doll's curls, "Home."

The plane came into sight and they were on third base, ready to steal home, when the sound of sirens joined the roar of private jet engines

"Up-oh," Rachel muttered, reaching under the seat for the satchel containing the Glock, the Beretta. "Looks like we have company."

Rand caught her hand. Shook his head.

"No. That's last resort. Here's what we do."

Though she was terrified by what the outcome might be if Rand's ploy didn't work, Rachel followed his instructions. They all piled out of the car—first Sarah and Montage, racing towards the plane, followed by her and Jayna.

She put the unloaded Beretta to Jayna's temple and pretended to drag her towards the plane along with the satchel while Rand approached several weapon-wielding officials, with one hand raised, the other holding onto a briefcase.

He spoke with what appeared be the man in charge.

From the safety of the plane, Rachel loaded the Beretta and wondered if she could actually start shooting real people, no matter how horrible they might be. She'd shot plenty of targets but never a human before. But as she watched Rand open the briefcase, she knew if the bribe wasn't accepted and they tried to take him away, she would literally kill for him in a heartbeat.

For heart palpitating seconds she watched the exchange...until the briefcase filled with counterfeit cash was accepted and the crooked cops got back into their cars, sirens silent as they drove away.

The hired backup peeled out and Rand made his way to join the group of escapees that were huddled together, no seat belts on before takeoff.

Rachel tossed the satchel and the Beretta she'd had trained on the local boss-man into the nearest cushy leather seat. She threw herself into Rand's arms the moment he reached the landing.

As a flight assistant slammed shut the door and the plane began to taxi down the runway, she covered his face with kisses.

She didn't even know she was crying until he stroked her wet cheeks with his thumbs, let her blow her nose into the same sleeve he had offered Sarah.

Shared snot on a sleeve. One that didn't come with initials.

She and Sarah already had something in common.

They loved the same man, for many of the same reasons, just in very different ways.

Once the sleek silver bird zoomed through the sky and Zebedique grew ever more distant, Rachel allowed herself a moment of utter and complete satisfaction.

She had a hand in all that she watched unfolding: Rand reunited with his sister. Sarah sobbing against his chest while she held onto a duplicate doll that he had given his concubine lover.

Sarah's doll had both eyes attached.

Rachel's attention shifted to Jayna and Montage, sharing what must be a very rare bottle of champagne, judging from their joyous, inebriated state of sisterhood as Jayna threw cards and Montage danced through the aisle trying to catch them, laughing gaily when the plane hit a pocket of air.

Rachel had no idea what fate might have in store upon their landing, but she did know this:

She would never in her life love a man as much as she loved Rand Slick.

And, if her period didn't start in two days, she was getting a pregnancy test *asap* to find out if she was responsible for more than returning a missing sister to a brother who lived 2500 miles away and no longer needed her in the capacity he'd hired her for.

Daddy had told her to always be careful when it came to mixing pleasure with business. He'd told her to keep her britches up and not to let him down. Not to give away free milk if you wanted a man to buy the cow.

And now that she'd given away enough milk to put Borden's Dairy out of business, there was one thing more Rachel knew:

In the unlikely event she was pregnant, she wouldn't tell Rand. That would be cheating. He had to want to buy the cow before she told him he was getting Elsie's whole damn farm.

CHAPTER 21

They no sooner touched ground at JFK than the circus came to town. Between arriving with two undocumented refugees, a kidnapped sister, turning evidence over to the FBI that wanted big dibs on an international sex trafficking operation, along with an exclusive expose in the New York Times that quickly caught fire with every major paper and magazine that wanted a piece of the action, everything was more than a little crazy.

Oh, and let him not forget Rachel taking Jayna back to Vegas with protective custodies in place, while he got Sarah and Montage settled in his New York penthouse.

The fact he had work piled up to an actual glass ceiling in his office while Rachel apparently didn't even have time to take most of his calls with her own phone ringing off the hook, had not worked in their favor.

A month had passed and they had not been completely alone, much less intimate, since their final night in Zebedique. Not exactly healthy for what had once been an extraordinary and deliciously robust sex life.

Rand didn't know if he should be worried, though obviously he was worried enough about the neglected state of their relationship to make a last minute trip to Vegas.

Rachel had offered to pick him up at the airport. He had declined. They had a lot to get settled in private and he didn't want their past due reunion publically exposed since the paparazzi had decided to get in on the circus act.

Enough had been uncovered about them both in the press that his real name, Joshua Smith, had been revealed. And much to his surprise, he honestly no longer cared. He was who he was and whatever name he went by didn't define him.

Rachel got all the credit for that personal epiphany.

Which in turn led to the credit he gave her for the attire he was wearing for this high stakes meeting. The clothes he had carefully selected didn't include a bespoke suit, Brioni tie, Allen Edmonds wing tips, or initials on the cuff of the best dress shirt money could buy.

But he had kept the cashmere socks, which cloaked the feet that entered a rundown building, his hopes climbing with each step ahead on threadbare carpet. He knew the PI he craved to smell, touch, and taste again was good. Make that exceptional.

Rand scanned the faded lettering on yellowed milk glass office doors until he stood in front of one that smelled of Windex. The black ink scored into clear beveled glass was carefully etched and still looked new.

"Rachel Tinsdale, Private Investigator," he whispered while his heart raced against the time closing in.

Rand gave himself a moment. Remembered. His stupid little stick-up act, her gun in his face, the pen he abrasively tossed to her desk, the money she handed him back. But what he remembered most of all was when she had asked him, *And just who are you, Mr. Slick?*

He was still figuring that out—who knew, maybe he had company with most everyone else on the planet with that proverbial question—but he did know that he was a very different man than the one who had stood in this same spot a mere few months ago.

A lot had changed since, and not just him. Rachel had changed, too. They had changed each other and they had changed together. But the last month had distanced them and it was a really bad feeling he had a dire need to correct—

Just like the shadier business practices that were no longer so shady. His indecent earnings had taken a substantial dip, but he was still a very wealthy man...though Rachel could swiftly reverse his fortunes if she decided that he just might be a little too high maintenance, which he was, and his manipulative instincts were still in prime working order, which they were, making her wary of agreeing to the kind of commitment he wanted from a witchy woman who liked to play it straight and always put her cards on the table.

Was she pregnant? If so, surely she would have told him. But if she was, and she hadn't, he fully intended to find out, and why not.

He stared at the office door, where a crucial answer waited on the other side.

Before Zebedique, where he would just barge in and claim some masterly rights, there had been another little ritual they'd shared. It was when he wondered if he was learning what love was, only for that question to culminate with Rachel's back against another door where he had softly banged her while a silver flask, a can of mace, and a Raggedy Ann with an eye missing had observed from her bookcase.

Shave-and-a-haircut-two-bits.

Rachel quickly gulped down the saltine cracker that came from a sleeve she'd nearly polished off and stuffed the evidence inside the schoolhouse desk she'd bought at the local St. Vincent DePaul's when she could barely afford cheap office rent.

"Come in," she called, hoping her lipstick was still intact and that Rand wouldn't notice her manicured nails were chewed down to some pretty unattractive nubs. Maybe the Tweed she'd dabbed on her neck and between her cleavage would divert his attention, along with the white vintage shirtdress she'd worn on their first meeting. The black patent belt still fit, along with matching pumps.

Her foot shook beneath the desk that was piled with inquiries and potential cases that kept pouring in while she longed for some champagne on ice that wouldn't upset her stomach or the current responsibility that took precedence in it.

The door to her office opened.

And there he was.

Rand wasn't wearing the hot business ensemble that had turned on every hormone she possessed upon their first meeting. He sported a nice pair of dark slacks, white Oxford shirt opened at the neck, and was approaching her desk in shoes that looked mighty fine but weren't the usual.

Eating her up with his gaze, he knocked her senseless with his slight smile and a cleanly shaven face that Gillette should invest in on the next Super Bowl commercial if they wanted to quadruple sales.

Rand deposited himself in the second hand wicker chair facing her second hand desk. His dark shuttered windows were in fine working order as they pulled her into their you-can-never-leave orbit.

"You look beautiful," he said without preamble. "Especially in that dress."

"Thank you."

"I've missed you."

"I've missed you more."

"Really? Then why haven't you returned more of my calls?"

Guilty as charged.

"Because I felt like we needed some space to get our acts together before we took on any elephants in the room."

"I see. Then let's tackle some of the niceties first. How is Jayna?"

"She's adapting well. I'm lucky to have her with me." *Ba-dump. Ba-dump.* "And how is Sarah, Montage?"

"Sarah's in therapy, making good progress. Montage can be a bit of a pain in the ass with her hovering, but she cooks a mean curry and takes good care of us both. It's not the kind of care I need, however. That would be from you."

Rachel didn't try to hide the pleasure in her smile, but neither did she pick up from where he'd left off. She was keeping that ball in his court as long as she could.

"Any chance you're missing the same kind of care from me?"

"I miss you every day, Rand."

"Then we need to figure out how to fix that for us both."

"Agreed, but 2500 miles between us doesn't make that exactly easy to figure or fix."

"Also agreed. So what do we do, meet in the middle and set up residence in Idaho?"

"Sure, why not?" She raised her hands, clapped them like a Flamenco dancer, jangling the charm bracelet on her wrist. "Let's just chuck it all and start a potato farm."

"Brilliant idea." He paused, tapped his sinfully kissable lips. Leaning forward, he asked, "Are you pregnant?"

Rachel blinked. Blinked again.

"Excuse me?"

"You heard me. Are. You. Pregnant?"

"What would make you ask me that?"

"I know what happened our last night together. I pretended sleep, but I was fully aware. Complicit and more than happy to oblige. If you're pregnant as a result, we both own it. Even if I have serious doubts about what kind of father I could ever be, I have none as to the kind of mother you would make."

Ba-dump. Ba-dump. Ba-dump!

"So...what are you saying?"

"I'm saying that if you're pregnant, we need to get ourselves to the nearest Reverend Elvis."

"And if I'm not?"

She held her breath. If Rand really loved her the way she loved him, he would propose, be willing to make that commitment, baby or no baby.

"Then I would like to propose that we share residences, give ourselves some time—especially you, you deserve that from me." Rand opened both palms to her, as if he had just made a very magnanimous gesture. One he spiked with, "There's plenty of room for us all in my penthouse. You can have the largest corner office in my company suites, plenty of room for your practice's expansion. Of course you could still maintain your office here in case you decide you need a break from me." His eyes lit up as if amazed by his own stroke of genius. "Just think, then you could legitimately say that you have offices coast-to-coast."

Legitimately. She wished he hadn't used that word.

Her galloping heart dropped like a stone into muddy water.

"Now let me be sure I have this straight." She really hoped she had misinterpreted something, somehow. Ba. Dump. "What you're basically saying is that if I'm preggers you'll step up to the plate and marry me. But if I'm not, you want us to shack up, mostly me shacking up with you. Knocked up equals Reverend Elvis. Not knocked up means bright lights, big city, and we're not talking neon on the strip. Have I got that right?"

Rand winced. "That sounds rather crude considering every-thing between us. But basically, yes."

As Rachel stared at this man she adored beyond adoring, so

delicious she could eat him up in his entirety then beg for seconds, thirds, not even a case of saltines could ease her sick stomach.

She wanted to puke.

And yet, she couldn't say he hadn't warned her that he was capable of disappointing her in some dreadful kind of way.

Mission accomplished.

Rachel rose from her second hand executive's chair and scoured Rand with a withering up and down assessment.

"You should leave now, Mr. Slick."

"But we just started talking," he responded as if they were brokering a polite business deal with some generous Détente provided on his end.

"No," she corrected. "We are through talking. I'm not pregnant. You're off the hook. And if you think for a single minute that I'll be agreeable to some kind of arrangement between your residence and mine so we can do what we apparently do best—like, mostly fuck and throw a little lovemaking into the mix to make it seem more *legitimate*—then *you* are sorely mistaken. I told you at the get-go that I wasn't easy."

"Of course not," he hastened to assure her. "I miss you, Rachel. I love you. I'm just trying to figure something out to make this work."

"Spoken like a Big Swinging Dick who traded his Allen Edmonds in for some boat shoes and a weekend shirt minus initials on the cuffs. I liked you better the other way. Put your suit back on, Rand, and that Brioni tie while you're at it. And don't come back until you're ready to buy the cow."

"What?"

"You heard me." Rachel left her desk, gave a little back kick with her heel to the chair he was sitting in, then breezed past him to open the office door where she pointed a forefinger exit. "Now get out."

Rand left the chair, as she had ordered. He went to the door she had opened and—

Firmly pushed it shut. Turned the deadbolt. Pulled down the shade over etched window glass.

"No," he countered. "I'm not going anywhere. And neither are you."

CHAPTER 22

*R*and had no idea why Rachel was so angry with him. He had tried to do the right thing and here she was throwing it all back into his face.

Hers was flushed, eyes flaring, he almost expected to see her hair catch fire. The way Rachel was flicking the bracelet on her wrist was so agitated he wondered if she was about to slap him—or give him his bracelet back.

He couldn't let that happen, at least not the bracelet part. This entire reunion was disintegrating in some seriously scary ways he was urgent to circumvent. Talking was getting them nowhere but dug deeper into whatever hole she wanted to throw him into, and this was a conversation that needed a new direction before more damage was done.

Rand gripped her flicking wrist with one hand, did the same with the other, and had them both over her head and against the wall before she could protest.

"Now," he told her, leaning in to pin her in place. "To say you smell divine and I want to bury my nose against your neck and anywhere else I can inhale you, is an understatement. But something else stinks here and I'm not sure what it is. Quite frankly, at the moment, I don't care. We can save discoverability for later. Right now, I have one intention and one intention only."

She turned her head so he couldn't kiss her.

Fine.

He'd always subscribed to the belief of adversity only being opportunity in disguise.

Nose to her neck and he knew she had worn the Tweed for him, the scent that made him feel secure as a child, and inebriated his senses as a man.

He tongued it up and felt the trip hammer of her jugular under his suckling mouth. Yes, definitely an improvement in their communication. Not to mention that he was even more starved for her than he'd realized. It was tempting to let go of her hands so he could put his all over her...

But not yet. Not until he was sure any hand roving would be reciprocal.

Just as he'd laid beneath her that last night they shared, and let her do as she pleased without participation or interference, she did the same now.

Fine, too.

They both knew how that turned out. He just hadn't expected to be so disappointed to learn she wasn't expecting his child.

Her skin, baby soft, was so familiar and yet new all over again. His own body against hers was thick with sense memory, with the stimulation of some long over-due contact that wasn't in the least diminished by the presence of their clothes.

"Spoken like a Big Swinging Dick who traded his Allen Edmonds in for some boat shoes and a weekend shirt minus initials on the cuffs. I liked you better the other way. Put your suit back on, Rand, and that Brioni tie while you're at it. And don't come back until you're ready to buy the cow."

What cow she was referring to, he didn't know, but he'd buy

any cow she wanted if that would make her happy. Even give it a room in his penthouse if she came along with it.

But the other, that hurt. It made him wish he hadn't told her about the term his status on Wall Street had earned, or the reason he wore those particular shoes. That was a confidence he had entrusted her with, and she had used it against him.

Rand took a sharp little bite of a delicate earlobe, pulled it through his bad wolf teeth.

Her sudden gasp was ferociously rewarding. He knew what she liked. And he wasn't above using it against her, either.

There was a place, on her interior arm, just above her biceps and below a ticklish pit, that had proven to be highly erogenous. With her arms raised in the white vintage dress with short cap sleeves, he had full access.

And while he was busy putting his mouth from one upper interior arm to the other, in just the right place judging from the little moans she was clearly struggling to contain but with limited success, he decided any hand roving didn't necessarily need to be reciprocal.

Down he pulled one pale, slender arm, skating his teeth against the interior until he reached a charm braceleted wrist. A soft bite into her palm. Hitch in her breathing. A not so soft bite. Double hitch. Forefinger tip to his mouth.

It was the same finger she had pointed him out the door with. Well, it wasn't exactly pointing him out anymore, now was it?

He was aware her nails weren't perfectly painted and filed; they were bare and shortened, which seemed a bit odd, but that didn't detract from the delectability of a tapered finger that tasted slightly of salt.

Up and down he sucked it in an imitation of their prolific coupling that had never been about mostly fucking—*why would she diminish them by saying something like that?*—but it was nevertheless a deep, essential, glorious part of their relationship that bound them together.

He sought to bind her closer as he brought the arm he still held captive above her head around his neck. Although her hand didn't sift through his hair or tease his nape, at least she didn't remove it.

Nor did she try to push him away when he reluctantly gave up a no longer salty finger, and lessened his full frontal lock against the wall to insinuate his hand over her stomach. Centered between her pelvis and slightly above the pubis was a very sweet spot that, when massaged just right, stimulated the G-spot externally with internal sensory consequences.

No, he wasn't letting any of his educational tools go to waste, not on your life.

He didn't hike up her skirt. Didn't delve past her panties or try to pull them down. Didn't need to.

Intent on sealing the deal they were brokering whether Rachel knew it or not, he insinuated a leg under her skirt and between hers.

They were trembling. Good. No hosiery, just his pants leg to a warm, moist cotton crotch. Excellent.

Then up and up he lifted, shifting into a slow rhythmic movement that escalated to keep time with her own involuntary thrusts. Her inner thighs gripped the one he had planted between her legs, and the sweet spot he continued to massage low in her belly made him realize how deeply he wanted his baby inside this woman who had changed him, made him want to be a man worthy of her love.

He could feel her holding off as long as she could until she turned her mouth to his.

For a moment he considered making her work for the kiss she was belatedly offering...

But he wasn't stupid, and took what he could never get enough of, not in a million years.

Ruby lips melted like clarified butter under his as he withdrew his hand from her stomach, and with two palms over the curvature of lush feminine hips, he ensured that Little Miss Red would all the better ride him.

He made her come, come to him, on the leg that rocked her, on the kiss he poured all that he felt for her into, and in that there was no end—

Until she was still and her thighs released their grip. Until he gave up her mouth and pressed his lips against the raven hair he threaded hungry fingers for her, and only for her, into.

"And now that we have this much settled between us, Ms. Tinsdale," he murmured, certain of a far better outcome than the gut-churning fear he'd experienced when she'd told him to get out, Rand moved slightly back. Tilted up her chin. Looked into puzzling pools of green. "Do you still want me to leave?"

He saw the indecision in her eyes...replaced by a look he recognized all too well.

He watched her slowly pivot. Even more slowly unlock the deadbolt.

Then decisively open the door.

Fine.

But he wasn't leaving without the final word.

He strode to her desk, tossed down the envelope with *TBD* inscribed on the front which he'd brought along to finalize their business agreement.

A Big Swinging Dick knew when to walk so a lesser player had no choice but to realize their mistake and come crawling back later, if it wasn't too late.

With Rachel, it would never be too late. But she had a lesson to learn and he was delivering it with the business card he extended at her open door.

She looked upset and that never failed to soften and move him, but when she said nothing and didn't take his card, he was fed up enough to skate it from her lips, down her throat, and tuck the card into her bodice.

Then he traced the wet spot she'd left on his trousers, made sure her eyes were on the evidence that they were anything but over even if he was all but out the door.

And departing on the terms he set forth: "When you're ready to come to your senses, call me."

By the time Rand got back to New York and the fragrant scent of curry emerging from the kitchen Montage had taken over, he had absolutely no appetite. Only great big question marks over his head and a hunger he couldn't appease since walking away from the most delicious dish in his life. Like final meal delicious.

"Joshua?"

"Hey, Angel."

"I'm glad you're home."

He thought once, twice, three times before saying, "Me, too," and hoped Sarah \bought his lie.

"How'd it go with Rachel?"

"Not so good."

Sarah gave him a much needed sisterly hug.

"I'm sorry. Want to talk about it?"

"Not really."

"Okay, but…maybe you should anyway."

Sarah sounded like a shrink. Maybe she was right. God knew he probably should have gotten himself to a reputable Dr. Freud years ago.

Rand availed himself of the impressive bar that was part of an open living area fronted by floor to ceiling glass overlooking the Manhattan skyline. The voluminous room spread out in various directions in a penthouse that claimed several thousand square feet of prime New York real estate.

Like any of it mattered when he'd be happier living with Rachel in a pup tent.

After pouring two fingers of Macallan 20 Year Scotch neat into Baccarat crystal, he planted himself on some very nice high end Italian leather and longed to be sitting on Rachel's worn tapestry couch where a bookcase stood sentry and a one-eyed Raggedy Ann doll knew what it was like to have an essential part missing.

Sarah sat beside him. She took the hand that wasn't tipping back the glass.

"What happened?"

He told Sarah most of it, leaving out the more intimate details.

"I see. So she showed you the door after you offered to take her to Reverend Elvis but the offer didn't stand if a baby wasn't involved."

"I didn't say it like that, didn't mean it like that." Another tip of Macallan's to his loose lips. He could trust Sarah, even if his trust in Rachel had hit a speed bump. "I offered her everything and she threw it back like I had insulted her. I have no idea where to go from here."

Sarah leaned in on his shoulder, took the crystal from his hand, then a little sip and wrinkled her nose.

"Well, I might. Do you have a special present you could send her? Something of sentimental value, just between you two, that no one else would really understand?"

Of course he did. He'd slept with it every night in Rachel's absence and wished he could take it to work, drag it around his offices like Linus with his blankie.

"Yes," was his answer.

"Then send it to her."

Sarah was a great sister, he was beyond grateful to have her back, all thanks to Rachel. But Sarah's advice, while no doubt sound, was like trying to decode Russian KGB intelligence.

Women.

"And then what do I do?"

"What you should have done in the first place."

"And what's that?"

Sarah took another sip of his Macallan's, shuddered, then gave the crystal containing it back.

"My best advice to you is to drink up, brother. We have some serious planning to do."

CHAPTER 23

"**F**ull house, Mistress! I won. Hand over the loot."

"Cripes, Jayna. You're wiping me out." Rachel shoved a pile of pennies over the spot they'd cleared on her desk. Even the bright shiny new ones looked like dull copper compared to Jayna's metallic gold lame jogging suit.

"It will go to a good place."

"More investments into Caesar's?"

"No, they take more than they give back. I will send it home."

Rachel thought of the contents in Rand's TBD envelope to settle up his debt. She had given into curiosity and found a banknote for a ridiculous $1M, along with something of more value—his bold script racing beneath corporate letterhead that read: *A small portion of all that I owe you. Love always, Rand*

It was the "Love always" that kept her from sending the envelope and its contents right back to him.

She was still sending most of the TBD back. But there was a good place a portion of that money could go.

"Jayna, I'm writing you a check." She did and handed it over to the kindest hands she had ever known. "Keep what you want for yourself and send the rest to your family."

Jayna's eyes practically bulged out of their sockets while she shook her head, beautiful silver streaked hair swishing over gold lame.

"I cannot accept this. It is too much."

"Of course you can accept it." Rachel thought of the note she had placed into safe keeping with a doll—and now a ceremonial bed sheet that had stolen her breath when it arrived beautifully presented in a carved box they had purchased at the Zebedique market. "It's just a small portion of all that we owe you. Especially me."

"But Mistress—"

"Please quit calling me that."

"Very well, Rachel, I will try. But only if you will listen to me and try, too."

Jayna laid down the check, reached across the pennies, and stilled the hand Rachel was finger-drumming.

"Call him. Tell him of the baby you carry. He will come."

"No. Absolutely not."

"But you are so sad."

"Heartbroken, Jayna."

"And stubborn." The understanding in her wise eyes contrasted with the chastisement of her voice. "You foolish woman. Why must you be so proud? The Master, he loves you."

"I know he does."

"Then what is stopping you?"

It was a question Rachel had been asking herself ever since the sheet had arrived. No note attached. It was hers and Rand's secret. No words needed to convey all that it symbolized.

She was being stubborn, prideful, she knew it. But for Chrissakes, why couldn't he have just said, "We'll get ourselves to Reverend Elvis, whether you're pregnant or not" instead of laying out some grand plan that would land her in a city as foreign to her as Zebedique, no wedding ring in sight, while she left everything and everyone that was familiar to pursue the kind of consuming career she didn't really want?

Of course she intended to be successful, build her practice. But there was more to life than juggling cases and making big money—like she needed it if she took his payoff, which she wasn't going to do—and turning into a slave of professional ambition. She wanted this baby. She wanted a family. She wanted a hard-headed man who was brutally handsome, that was more committed to her than life in the fast lane.

"That's a good question, Jayna. I thought I knew but I'm no longer so sure."

"Then call him."

"I'll think about it," Rachel conceded. And then she thought of how selfish she was being—yeah, her and Rand, they had more in common than not—and clasped Jayna's patting hand. "How are you doing, Jayna, being so far away from your family now? Sorry, I've been too wrapped up in my own elephant poop to even ask lately."

"I miss them, but I have no regrets. Montage and I talk, and that helps. She is my good friend. But Rachel, you are my family here. And I look forward to holding your little one when it comes."

"You'll make a great nanny, Jayna." Rachel glanced at the piles of inquiries on her desk, the phone she'd turned off next to Jayna's carefully printed call back notes. Between the morning sickness and exhaustion since she couldn't seem to get enough sleep, she may as well be clocked out for most of the day while Jayna picked up the slack. She was an ace assistant.

One who was going to the window that her daddy probably would have thrown Rand Slick out of during that first meeting... and would want to shake hands with now.

Guts. Daddy would be impressed with the man who sure knew

how to steal a woman's heart and step up to the plate after she'd gotten herself pregnant. *What had she been thinking?* That was the question she'd asked herself when the results came in, but she'd known it the moment she made such a fateful decision.

They had been heading into an uncertain future and if for some reason things didn't work out with Rand, if the client decided he no longer needed the doctor that had been thinking with her britches, then she would have a part of him forever that she had stolen and he could never steal back.

"I pretended sleep, but I was fully aware. Complicit and more than happy to oblige. If you're pregnant as a result, we both own it. Even if I have serious doubts about what kind of father I could ever be, I have none as to the kind of mother you would make."

Wait.

More than happy to oblige...we both own it.

Why was that part of what he'd said just now getting sifted out of all the other blah, blah, blah she'd been listening to instead?

Jayna drew the window blinds. Returned to the desk, gave Rachel a hug.

"You should rest. I have some things to do and will be back."

"Take the day off, Jayna. You've been working overtime to cover for us both. I'll meet you at home later."

"Very well, Mis—" Catching herself, Jayna said, "Rachel. See, I am trying. You should try too. Call him."

And with that last bit of advice, Jayna left.

Rachel fingered the business card Rand had tucked inside her bra.

Her breasts were getting bigger. She'd have to buy some new bras soon. New wardrobe, too. It wouldn't be long and all her cute little vintage numbers would be replaced by elasticized pants and circus tent dresses to accommodate the company her stomach was now keeping.

Now. What a loaded word. She'd once thought that Now didn't care about tomorrow, but she'd been wrong. Now was like a domino that set all the ones to follow into motion, and if she looked ahead to how those dominoes would best fall, even if they didn't all line up and perfectly meet her expectations, then she could make a move in this very moment that would cut through all the bullshit Rand had been trying to shovel up while she just piled it right on.

Jayna was right. Time to woman up.

Deep breath. She reached for the phone.

The door to her office swung open, no knock. Door shutting; click of a deadbolt. Shade pulled over etched window.

"I'm looking for a missing person."

Hotel California eyes and a Gillette ad copy jawline, along with a bespoke suit that came with all the Rand Slick GQ fixings, pinned her where she sat as he purposefully strode to the other side of antiquated oak.

He promptly withdrew a black velvet box from his pocket, opened it, and landed a diamond ring the size of Egypt on top of the pennies Jayna had left on her desk.

Rand trained a forefinger on her with the unquestionable authority of the barrel of a gun.

"You," he said with no further ado. "You are the person I'm missing, Ms. Tinsdale. I'm no bargain, that's for sure, but if you'll have me, I want to marry you. Reverend Elvis is just down the street. We can do it now, or take a few days and do it a little more right with some special attendees to join us. Just don't take too long to decide since I have no intentions of sleeping another night without you."

It was a lot to take in.

Rachel tried to say something and she could feel her lips moving but nothing was coming out of her mouth.

The man who had just proposed didn't wait for the words that weren't emerging. He came around the desk, pulled her to feet that felt like they were levitating while the head she tilted back had the substance of helium. Just when she thought he was going to kiss her, Rand veered from her mouth, skated some big bad wolf teeth up the side of her neck, and whispered into her ear, "*Say yes.*"

"Yes." Rachel kissed him harder than she'd ever kissed him before, disengaging only long enough to shout, "Yes!"

Had Jayna told Montage and had Montage told Sarah only for Sarah to tell Rand he was going to be a daddy?

Rachel didn't care. Smart mothers-to-be didn't put pride before knowing what love was and accepting the trade-offs of not always having it their own way.

"Then we've got a deal. The for better or worse lifetime kind. Unfortunately you're probably getting the worse, but I'll make up for that wherever I can. I love you, Rachel. When I look at you, it's like staring at the sun too long and I love you blind. I want us to make babies, have a family. I don't care where. I know we still have a lot to figure out, but getting this ring on your finger is the first right step in our TBD direction."

Vegas wasn't necessarily the best place to raise kids, even though she truly appreciated and loved the carnival, the neon color of life that consisted of casinos, strippers, Liberace and more that had composed her raising. As for New York, she'd never been there, but from what she knew the two cities that never slept had a lot in common. One was just more sophisticated, cultured, and had Wall Street with Big Swinging Dicks instead of betting pools, bookies, and female impersonators that made Cher look better in drag than she could pull off herself.

Idaho was starting to look good.

"We'll figure it out." Rachel glanced at the ring that was awfully damn impressive even though a cigar band would have secured her agreement. "I have something to tell you, Rand."

"I'm happy with 'Yes.' Anything else you have to say is icing on top of the wedding cake."

"You're going to be a father." She extended the jewelry box, its outrageous contents glistening from the middle. "Now you can put a ring on it."

She watched his Adam's apple move up and down. Saw the glistening in his eyes, but of course he didn't cry.

"You should have told me."

"Yes, I should have."

"Why didn't you?"

Rachel considered his question, knew she wasn't happy with her truthful response.

"Because I wanted you to buy the cow first." Trying to find some justification for it, she explained, "It's just the way I was raised."

"A father," he whispered. Extracting the ring from the box, he promptly slid it down her finger and whooped, "A father! Elvis here we come!"

They made a complete mess of her desk.

As they held each other tighter than tight, his leavings between her thighs just in case they needed to double down, Rand fingered the bracelet at her wrist.

"Any more questions before we do this?"

"Yes. Just one." Rachel pinged the mysterious charm that came at the end of delicate links, beside the clasp. "What's with the thimble? Everything else makes sense, except for this thimble I still haven't figured out."

"Oh, but that's the easiest one of all." Rand's windows were fully open, waving her inside as he pressed her hand against his heart. "Rachel, you mend me."

bookmark:Epilogue

EPILOGUE

TWENTY YEARS LATER - THE SNAKE RIVER VALLEY, IDAHO

The sun was just setting when Joshua Smith, Jr. looked out over rolling acres of grape vines that would become more award-winning Riesling, and knew if he could look further in one direction he would see endless acres of potato crops that were irrigated by snowmelt running off the Teton Mountains, while in the other direction he would see herds of American Wagyu cattle, raised for some of the finest restaurants coast-to-coast that served their family's signature Kobe-style beef.

"Dad, I've decided that I really don't want to go."

"I'm sorry, son, I know how much you love the farm, but it's important that you finish your college education. Don't forget, we struck a deal, and if I've taught you anything it's that—"

"A man is only as good as his word."

Josh looked at the man he could meet eye-to-eye now, but he would never stop looking up to a father that was Superman as far as he was concerned—tall enough to leap skyscraper buildings and outrun any train. The speeding bullet part, though, that went straight to his mom.

He didn't know how she did it, raising three kids—him, Dolly, and Joseph, who'd been named after the grandfather that had passed before any of them were born—and overseeing one of the largest ranches in Idaho with his dad. She even took on an occasional missing person case if it really spoke to her.

His mother was fairly petite, especially compared to him and his look-alike dad—Dolly took after their mom—but nobody ever doubted who was running the show at the Smith Family Farm. It was really a ranch with vast swaths of land, but for some reason she liked to call it a farm—though "damn farm" got used a lot too.

"I'd like to negotiate on that deal we struck, Dad."

"Oh?" A salt-and-pepper eyebrow lifted. "Then let's see what kind of negotiation skills you have."

Josh knew he was about to take on one of the shrewdest businessmen in the state, if not the whole country, but hey, he'd learned from the best.

He didn't want any interruptions so he turned off his cell phone.

His father nodded, did the same.

"Well, you know that Jayna's really getting up there."

"Yes." A pause. "Not that being in her eighties has slowed her down. Or Montage."

Intercepted at the gate.

"Of course. But you also know that Aunt Sarah and Uncle Craig count on me to help watch the cousins when they want to go out to dinner or something and Montage is off on one of those cruises she likes to take with Jayna."

"I know you're the favorite babysitter, but Dolly and Joseph are driving now and I'm sure they'll be happy to step in."

"Maybe so, but when it comes to potato harvesting season, all they want to do is go ride some horses instead of pulling their weight on a tractor." He loved harvesting season, loved it enough to sacrifice a second one this sophomore year if it meant he didn't have to give up another one again. It fell along the lines of the sign his parents had hung directly over their refrigerator: *Anything truly worth having often comes at some personal cost. There is no free lunch.*

Dad stroked his jaw, the way he did when he was considering. "We have plenty of hired help that regard tractor riding, and all the other things the farm requires, their job."

"I know. But it's not their land. It's ours and we have an obligation to it to get our hands in the dirt and our backs sore, too." Crossing his arms, Josh went toe-to-toe with the master negotiator. Even their mom slipped and called him "Master" sometimes. "I would like to propose that if I pull a 4.0 this semester at Wharton, then I can transfer to Idaho State to finish out my degree. In agriculture."

Now his father frowned. Forehead wrinkled. He looked him really close in the eyes, but Josh didn't blink. Like father, like son, he wasn't going to back down.

"I thought you wanted to go to Wharton. Get a business degree."

If his father had taught him one thing about the art of negotiation, it was the surprising power of honesty.

"I know you thought that, Dad. You thought it because I wanted to think it myself. But the truth is that I wanted to please you by earning the degree you never had a chance to get. I wanted to make you proud."

His father did something he never did when it came to business. He blinked.

Just then, with the worst timing possible, a jeep came careening their way, horn honking a loud "Shave-and-a-haircut-two-bits" knock, followed by an "Ooooga."

Why his parents thought it was funny to install that kind of sound effect on a jeep's horn beat him. So was the way they liked to change the sheets together every now and then with his dad wearing a suit while his mom put on some really old clothes, like from the 50's, and they cranked the music up, always playing songs from The Eagles.

Weird.

Especially since the whole family mostly wore jeans, work shirts and boots unless they were going to some kind of fund raiser function or traveling out of the country, which he didn't particularly enjoy since he was a home boy, and home was here.

Bounding out of the jeep, his mom ran their way. With that red hair of hers flying sometimes she looked like a witch, a really pretty one, just minus the broom.

"Rand! Joshua! I tried to call but...damn reception out here. We have company. Uncle Jack flew in from Vegas and decided to pay us a surprise visit." She gave Josh a little kiss on his cheek. A big kiss on his dad's mouth.

Those two. His parents didn't argue often but when they did, *whew.* Could they have some doozies—that didn't last nearly as long as what his dad called Détente, when they settled their differences in private.

As if realizing she had walked in on a man-to-man between father and son, his mother stepped back, sized them both up.

"Sorry," she said. "Did I interrupt something, show up at a bad time?"

His dad looked from her to him.

"Actually your timing couldn't have been better." He put an arm around her, then slapped Josh on the back. "We were just discussing how Joshua's going to sit out this semester so he can help with the harvest. He's changing majors and enrolling at Idaho State where he'll pick his education back up next year."

Score! Joshua fist pumped the fresh Idaho air where rolling acres of grapes and potatoes and herds of cattle were nestled between majestic Teton mountains and Snake River water. Where he would keep his end of the bargain by getting the education his father never had, and in exchange he would work his way up to step in when his parents were ready to retire.

"That's wonderful!" his mother exclaimed.

"Indeed it is," his father agreed. And with a look of admiration that Josh knew he would never, ever forget, came the final pronouncement from a man who stood so tall in his eyes, that he could hang the moon that rose paper white above them: "Our son is quite the negotiator. And I couldn't be prouder of him." A firm handshake to seal the deal. "He's got guts."

The End

LOVE LESSONS

RISKY LOVERS, BOOK 2

"More champagne for my bride?"

"Yes, please." As Eric topped off her flute, Whitney eyed the rest of the bottle and wondered if there was enough courage in it for what remained of the night.

"The way you say that, I'm given to wonder if you're actually nervous about going to bed with your husband."

Was she? Eric had sent the villa's staff home early; she'd been hoping they would work late. But instead of blurting, "Of course I'm nervous!" Whitney managed to explain, "I've never had a husband before, Eric. Everything just feels different."

"Bad different?" He removed his cufflinks. She gave a little jump at the soft clatter of his jewelry hitting the glass table where an exquisite tiered cake was parked. "Or, good different?"

"Yes. No. Both." She took another sip. "I don't know."

"Whitney, look at me."

Eric had left his chair, was kneeling in front of her. Despite feeling a little ridiculous for her behavior, she knew something was different. Eric had expectations. Their relationship had shifted from her "we'll see's" and "maybe's" to a more profound kind of ground.

"I love you," he said simply, as if those three words were the only ones needed in an unsettled world to bridge whatever chasms might divide it. "We took vows today. Even if you decide later that you'd rather throw yourself into traffic than be married to me, tonight I need your assurance that you don't regret it already." He leaned in, but didn't try to kiss her. "I said I wouldn't ask, but I'm asking anyway. Would you tell me what I've been waiting to hear?"

Whitney touched his cheek. "How could you ever doubt it?"

"I don't." He pressed his lips into her palm. "I just need to hear you say it."

"I love you." The words that had been bottled up came out in a whispered rush. And once released, they couldn't stop coming. "I love you, I love you. Love you."

"That's exactly what I needed to hear. From my Whitney. My yuan-pau." He extended his hand and as she interlocked her fingers with his, Eric significantly concluded with, "But I especially needed to hear it from my wife."

He rose, pulling her up with him, then tilted her head to study her face. His own wore an expression that conveyed the same glittering intelligence that had slightly unnerved her earlier, but now it was infiltrated with a raw yearning that caused her to feel the same fight or flight instinct summoned by a dark stranger who had the courtesy to knock before barging in.

The dark stranger she had married kissed her. In all the kisses they had shared before she had never quite felt that Eric had made it his mission to suck her into his orbit so completely that she had no means of escape; nor the desire for it.

That's when she realized. Eric had set a velvet trap: He had told her what he knew she needed him to say before she would sign those papers and walk down that aisle.

It was the ultimate bait and switch: He had reeled her in on a three-month agreement. And while she had been strategizing for an early exit if necessary, his sole purpose was to ensure that she never left.

Eric could taste the flavor of her shifting responses, her emotions. And he could certainly discern the effect it was all having on her physically.

Whitney was trembling. So were the lips she kept partially closed, like gates that weren't completely shutting him out but neither were they providing full entrance.

It didn't take a genius to know that she was afraid—and it wasn't completely unwarranted. After all, throughout the entire business of getting married, he had known something that Whitney seemed to just now be grasping.

All of their previous interactions and intimacies fell into the category of: Before. Official papers, a ring, the vows they had taken, bore the distinct designation of: After.

No doubt Whitney's anxiety was fueled by making a legal commitment to a man she knew, but didn't fully know. And yet that was part of the mystery of marriage: That two people could grow and change together, that there was one person bearing witness to your strengths, your foibles, your transitions in life, and part of your pact was to hold each other accountable while being more supportive and compassionate than anyone else in the world when either of you failed.

If one learned more from their failures than their successes, he knew a lot about marriage.

He and Whitney had been like children playing. Now they had crossed a line. Marriage was for adults. Time to grow up.

Putting the kiss on pause that she wasn't wholeheartedly

returning, Eric considered how to get this honeymoon night on track.

"I have another gift for you. But first, let's refill that flute."

"Thank you, Eric."

Her relief was so palpable he wondered if maybe he should get her tanked. They could laugh years later about a wedding night when their greatest intimacy was him holding up her hair so it didn't join any miserable prayers over porcelain.

"Here's to you, Mrs. Townsend." He tapped his crystal to hers. "Here's to us."

Whitney looked from her glass with the last remains of her lipstick, to him, as if debating between an AA meeting and throwing her lot in with a wine wielding Bacchus.

"There's no rush," he assured her. "As much as I'd love to slip you out of that dress and into nothing for a proper commemoration, I am completely okay with just hanging out tonight."

"What about tomorrow?"

"Maybe you'll make out with me while we watch a movie."

Now she was smiling. "And the day after?"

"My patience will be completely worn out. Even ten pairs of Nikes hitting ground at full speed won't stand a chance of you outrunning me." He reached around her back, slipped his hand beneath the scooped fabric, and unhooked her bra. "So, what might I grant my wife on our wedding night? More Dom? Cake? Pizza?" A pause and he hopefully added, "Me?"

"I think we need to get naked."

"Do you?" He inclined his head, appearing to consider. "Why?"

"Honestly, Eric, nothing has felt familiar today and I could use some familiar ground. I'm thinking once we're back in bed, where we have spent an awful lot of time, things will feel more normal."

He softly laughed at her naiveté, at his own before Whitney had turned everything he thought he knew about life and love on its head. She had taught him more in six weeks than he had learned in three decades. His wife—yes, his wife—was a gifted teacher. Hopefully she would deem her husband not too shabby himself.

"We can get as naked as we were yesterday, and all the days before," he told her. "But it won't be the same."

"No?"

"No." He kissed the wedding ring he had put on her finger, then led his willing bride towards the bedchamber door. "It'll be better."

Available in paperback or ebook from your favorite bookstore or online retailer.

ABOUT THE AUTHOR

Mallory Rush believes in true love's ability to elevate all of our lives from the ordinary to the transcendent. As Olivia Rupprecht she has written and edited fiction and non-fiction, and was series developer for the True Vows reality-based romance series from HCI Books. Writing as Hart Rivers, she is also co-author of the bestselling Murder on the Mekong series of psychological thrillers. But when it comes to romance, she considers it to be more than a storytelling genre—it's as essential as breathing for a truly rich life. Mallory loves to hear from her readers.

www.MALLORYRUSH.com
www.murderonthemekong.com

www.ingramcontent.com/pod-product-compliance
Lightning Source LLC
Chambersburg PA
CBHW050420260626
47156CB00003B/1088